Also by Claudia Mills

Losers, Inc.
Standing Up to Mr. O.
You're a Brave Man, Julius Zimmerman
Lizzie at Last
Alex Ryan, Stop That!
Perfectly Chelsea
Makeovers by Marcia
Trading Places
The Totally Made-up Civil War Diary of Amanda MacLeish
One Square Inch

claudia mills

ZERO TOLERANCE

SQUARE
FISH

Farrar Straus Giroux
New York

To Cat Kurtz

SQUARE
FISH

An Imprint of Macmillan
175 Fifth Avenue
New York, NY 10010
mackids.com

ZERO TOLERANCE. Copyright © 2013 by Claudia Mills.
All rights reserved. Printed in the United States of America by
R. R. Donnelley & Sons Company, Harrisonburg, Virginia.

Square Fish and the Square Fish logo are trademarks of Macmillan and
are used by Farrar Straus Giroux under license from Macmillan.

Square Fish books may be purchased for business or promotional use.
For information on bulk purchases, please contact the Macmillan
Corporate and Premium Sales Department at (800) 221-7945 x5442 or
by e-mail at specialmarkets@macmillan.com.

Library of Congress Cataloging-in-Publication Data
Mills, Claudia.
  Zero tolerance / Claudia Mills.
    p. cm.
  "Margaret Ferguson books."
  Summary: Seventh-grade honor student Sierra Shepard faces
expulsion after accidentally bringing a paring knife to school,
violating the school's zero-tolerance policy.
  ISBN 978-1-250-04422-8 (paperback) / ISBN 978-0-374-38832-4
(e-book)
  [1. Middle schools—Fiction. 2. Schools—Fiction.] I. Title.

PZ7.M63963Ze 2013   [Fic]—dc23   2012017851

Originally published in the United States by Farrar Straus Giroux.
First Square Fish Edition: 2014
Book designed by Jay Colvin
Square Fish logo designed by Filomena Tuosto

10 9 8 7 6 5 4 3 2 1

AR: 5.2 / LEXILE: 670L

ZERO TOLERANCE

1

Sierra Shepard sat in the office at Longwood Middle School during lunch recess 5A, waiting to see her principal, Mr. Besser. She adjusted her red plaid skirt so that it draped neatly over her knees and tucked a strand of shoulder-length brown hair back into her matching headband. Outside in the hallway, some kids peered in through the glass windows to see who was in trouble this time. She could tell that they were disappointed when they saw that she was the one sitting there.

Oh, it's just Sierra.

Above her head hung the banner she had helped sew with the other seventh-grade members of the Longwood Leadership Club. Letters cut from different-colored squares of fabric were appliquéd onto a large white cloth rectangle, spelling out the four words that formed the Longwood Middle School creed:

RULES
RESPECT
RESPONSIBILITY
RELIABILITY

It still bothered Sierra that the fourth "R," the one in RELIABILITY, was slightly crooked. She had wanted to tell Em to snip it off and sew it on again more carefully, but Celeste had already been acting so bossy and critical that Sierra hadn't wanted to sound that way herself.

She would have brought the banner home and fixed the crooked "R" without saying anything. But Mrs. Frederick, who had been the Leadership Club adviser ever since Sierra had joined in sixth grade, had already started folding up the banner to take home to press. So now the "R" was crooked forever.

The "R" in RELIABILITY was unreliable.

The door to the office opened—not the door into Mr. Besser's inner sanctum, but the door that led out into the hall. Two boys entered—Luke Bishop and another kid Sierra didn't know. They were herded by a playground lady who wasn't exactly dragging them by their collars— touching students wasn't allowed—but who was keeping them in line with her scowl.

Sierra drew herself even more upright and looked down at the folder that she held in her lap.

The playground lady turned to Ms. Lin, one of the two school secretaries.

"Fighting," she said. "Again."

"He started it," the other boy spat out.

Luke sneered.

"I don't care who started it," Ms. Lin said.

The playground lady turned on her heel and marched away, as if relieved to be done with the unpleasant duty of delivering them to the office.

Ms. Lin pointed to the appliquéd banner. It really was useful to have it hanging right there.

"Rules," she read. "You boys know what the rule is about fighting at school. The rule is that all students involved in a fight are punished by in-school suspension. *All* students."

Luke dropped down into the chair directly next to Sierra, and the other boy into the chair next to him. Sierra thought about getting up and shifting into the remaining empty chair on the other side of her, but that might look rude, and Luke, who wasn't dumb even though he was in trouble all the time, might say something rude back.

He already called her by her last name instead of her first name, changing it to "Shep-turd." The only class they had together was health. Sierra was in honors classes for everything else, but there was no honors section for health. Luke had called her by that hideous name one day in health class, and some of the other not-so-good students had laughed.

Luke leaned over and said, "What did *you* do?"

At first Sierra didn't even understand the question. Then she got it. Was Luke joking?

"I didn't *do* anything!"

Luke glanced around the office as if to say, *Then why are you here?* He was one of the tallest seventh-grade boys, broad-shouldered, the kind of boy who would have been on the football team if his grades had been good enough to allow him to play. His long dark hair fell over one eye, and his T-shirt was torn, maybe from the playground fight with the other boy, who sat staring straight ahead.

"I'm here to talk to Mr. Besser about an idea I had— that the Leadership Club has—for a new school program."

It was actually Sierra's father's idea—he had read about it somewhere and told her about it—but then she had taken it to the Leadership Club, and they had thought it sounded great. The program was called ZAP, for Zeroes Aren't Permitted. Any kid who didn't turn in an assignment had automatic detention that day in a special study hall until he or she got the assignment done. That way no one ever got behind, and lots of kids who were failing wouldn't fail.

Luke gave a snort of contempt. Sierra clutched the folder that had her typed-up notes explaining this new idea.

"How do you know it's not a great program?" she asked him. "Actually, it's a program designed to help kids like you."

Luke gave her a look of such fury that she wondered if he might have attacked her physically if they hadn't been sitting outside the principal's office under Ms. Lin's watchful eye.

And then she, Sierra, would be in trouble for fighting! Because the rule said "No fighting," and it didn't matter who started it. Which did seem unfair, come to think of it. It would hardly have been Sierra's fault if Luke attacked *her*. It was hardly the other boy's fault if Luke had attacked *him*.

"Don't do me any favors, Shep-turd," Luke snarled.

Sierra wanted to snap back at him, *Maybe there isn't any program that could help a kid like you.*

But Ms. Lin called over to them, "No talking!" She gave Sierra an apologetic smile, clearly to let her know that the command was addressed to Luke, not her.

The other office door opened, and Mr. Besser stuck his bald head out. A lot of kids made fun of Mr. Besser for being bald—he made fun of it himself—but Sierra liked how he looked, with his bright eyes and waggling, bushy eyebrows.

Mr. Besser scanned the lineup of kids in their hard plastic chairs. He gave the two boys a stern stare. He gave Sierra a friendly wink.

"Sierra was here first," Ms. Lin said.

"All right, Miss Shepard, come on in," Mr. Besser said. "Tell me what I can do for you today."

As Sierra accepted the principal's invitation to follow

him into the inner sanctum, she heard Luke mutter something. She was glad that she couldn't make out the words.

After her short meeting with Mr. Besser, who had promised he would give the ZAP idea "serious consideration," Sierra hurried to her locker to get her lunch. At Longwood Middle School, the lunch period was divided into an eating part and a recess part. Sierra had recess 5A and ate lunch 5B. So did her friends Emma Williamson, Lexi Kruger, and Celeste Vogel, which was lucky.

Sierra opened her locker, glancing at the things she had taped to the inside of her door—a picture of snow falling on the mountains that she had made in art class last semester, some goofy pictures of her and Em taken at a photo booth in the arcade at the mall, a printout of her goals for the semester, which she had made just over three weeks ago, on New Year's Day: *Speak up more in class. Read a library book every week. Don't let people push you around.* "People" meant Celeste. *Get more involved in Leadership Club.* She had done that one already, with her ZAP idea. *Don't think so much about B.* "B" meant "boys."

And "boys" meant Colin Beauvoir, who was in her accelerated language arts class, her math class, and her French class, as well as in the Octave, the elite eight-student a cappella choir that practiced Tuesday and Thursday mornings before school. Colin with the dreamy gray eyes and the slow, shy smile. Sierra loved the way his hands trembled just a little bit when he had to read aloud in class.

Sierra grabbed her insulated lunch bag and slammed her locker shut. She was definitely doing better at *Get more involved in Leadership Club* than at *Don't think so much about B.*

The noise level in the cafeteria was deafening as Sierra headed to the table by the window where her friends sat every day. She had thought Celeste wouldn't be back yet from getting her braces tightened, but there she was, her long, straight blond hair easy to see even from across the room. Tiny, smart-mouthed Lexi sat next to her; brainy, bookish Em was sitting across from them.

Sierra sat down next to Em.

"Do your braces hurt?" she asked Celeste sympathetically.

Celeste nodded. "But look." She flashed her smile; Sierra saw that Celeste's braces were now blue, the same blue as her eyes. "I got sick of pink. Pink is so last semester, don't you think?"

Sierra knew Celeste was joking, pretending to be a big authority on fashion. But Celeste definitely was a big authority on a lot of things.

"Did you talk to Besser?" Celeste asked Sierra.

"Uh-huh."

"And?"

"He said that ZAP was a great idea, and he'd give it serious consideration." Sierra felt herself beaming.

"Grownups say that when they're not going to do anything," Celeste said.

Sierra was glad to see Lexi give Celeste a withering look. All three girls were in Leadership Club with Sierra.

"Well, they do," Celeste said. "I'm just saying."

Lexi crumpled up her sandwich wrapper into a small, hard sphere and tried to toss it into the trash can, the way the boys did. She missed.

"Are you just going to leave it there?" Sierra asked.

"I'll get it when the bell rings. On my way out." As if registering Sierra's disapproval, Lexi added, "Look, it's not like it's going anywhere."

Sierra hopped up and walked the ten feet to the trash can, collected Lexi's wrapper, and disposed of it properly.

"You can't stand for a piece of litter to be on the floor for half a minute," Lexi teased when Sierra sat back down at the table.

"You shouldn't make Sierra throw away your trash for you," Celeste scolded.

"I didn't make her do anything. It's not my fault if Sierra's so anal."

Sierra knew that "anal" was a psychological term for someone who was compulsively neat and organized, which she was—well, neat and organized, not *compulsively* neat and organized. She hated the word, though. It made her think of Luke's nickname for her.

"Aren't you going to eat your lunch?" Celeste asked Sierra.

Sierra wasn't really hungry; she was too busy mentally

replaying her conversation with Mr. Besser. And, unlike the grownups of Celeste's apparent acquaintance, she knew that Mr. Besser did mean what he said.

Celeste never seemed to want to give anybody else in Leadership Club credit for having good ideas. It was one of the most annoying things about her. Sierra had become friends with Celeste mainly because they were the only two seventh-grade girls singing in the Octave; Colin was the only seventh-grade boy.

Sierra opened the Velcro flap on her lunch bag. Hungry or not, she'd better eat something, or her stomach might start rumbling in French class, right as she was sitting next to Colin.

She opened her sandwich and was about to take the first bite when she looked at it more closely. It was *ham* and cheese, not plain cheese. She must have grabbed her mother's identical lunch bag by mistake: Sierra hadn't eaten ham or pork or bacon ever since reading *Charlotte's Web* back in third grade.

"Great," she said. "I took my mother's lunch, and she took mine."

Irritated, Sierra dumped the contents of the lunch bag out onto the table. The loathsome sandwich, two oatmeal raisin cookies, an apple, and a paring knife to cut it with.

Sierra stared at the knife as if a coiled serpent had appeared from her mother's lunch bag, poised and ready to spring.

"Uh-oh," Lexi said.

"No weapons" was the biggest rule of all the rules at Longwood Middle School. No guns, not even toy guns. No knives, not even plastic knives.

For the first time since Sierra had come to the table, Em spoke up. "Just put it back in your lunch bag. It was your mother's knife, not yours. No one's seen it but us."

Lexi, who couldn't be bothered to pick up her own trash, quickly snatched the knife and stuck it back in the lunch bag, safely out of sight.

"It was just a mistake," Em said. "You took the wrong lunch. It could happen to anyone."

Celeste didn't say anything.

"No," Sierra said. "The rule says 'no knives.' Period. Not 'no knives unless you have them by mistake.' Or 'no knives except if they're not very sharp.' I'll take it over to the lunch lady, and she can put it in the kitchen or in the office, and my mom can come and get it when she picks me up after school."

Before she could change her mind, Sierra gathered up the rest of the contents of her lunch, put them back in the bag, and got up from the table. Carrying the lunch bag with the knife inside, she walked over to Sandy, the lunch lady.

She would explain everything to Sandy.

And then everything would be all right.

2

Sandy presided over the Longwood Middle School cafeteria. She was about the same age as Sierra's parents, maybe a little bit older, and definitely a lot heavier. Sandy never got off her stool unless there was a major spill or an outright brawl. She was generally good-natured, but you didn't want to be the kid who made Sandy have to get off her stool and actually do something rather than calling out the same ineffectual reprimands: "No running!" "No pushing!" "Keep it down, kids!"

"Yeah?" Sandy asked when Sierra approached her stool, lunch bag in hand.

"I took my mother's lunch by mistake," Sierra said.

Sandy didn't appear to be impressed. "So? Can't you just eat it?"

"But—"

"Look, by the time you call home, lunch'll be over with. We're talking five minutes until the bell."

"No, I mean, I can eat it"—well, not the ham on the sandwich—"but she had an apple, and—"

"No running!" Sandy yelled to a boy who was racing over to the conveyor belt with his tray. "What's wrong with an apple?"

Sierra opened up the lunch bag and extended it so that Sandy could see the knife, visible next to the sandwich and cookies. "She had this to cut it with."

Sandy's eyes widened. "You're not supposed to have that at school."

"I *know*. That's why I'm giving it to you."

Instead of simply accepting the knife—as if even a grownup weren't allowed to touch such a forbidden object—Sandy slipped down off her stool.

"Look, I can't leave these kids alone. Take that thing to the office. Just go there directly. Do you hear me?"

Despite her insistent tone, Sandy looked worried. Sierra could tell that she was wondering whether she'd get in more trouble if she abandoned her post in the cafeteria or if she let a weapon-wielding student walk unsupervised through the halls.

"Margie!" Sandy called over to one of the ladies behind the counter. "Margie, hold the fort for me, will you? I've got a situation."

Sierra winced at the word.

"Come with me," Sandy said.

When they arrived at the office, Ms. Lin looked up and started to give Sierra an automatic smile, but the expression on Sandy's face caused the smile to vanish before it had reached past the corners of her mouth, well before it had reached her eyes.

"She brought a knife to school," Sandy said to Ms. Lin.

"I *didn't*. I didn't even know I had it until—"

"Show her," Sandy ordered.

"It's my mother's knife. I took her lunch by mistake."

As the two women stared at her—glared at her?—Sierra had no choice but to reach in the lunch bag, pull out the knife, and set it down on Ms. Lin's desk.

Ms. Lin gave an audible gasp. The other secretary, Mrs. Saunders, looked up from her computer.

"I guess you can take it from here," Sandy said. "I'd better get back to our little darlings before someone gets killed."

It felt like a strange joke to make with a knife lying right there in plain view.

Just then the bell for the end of 5B sounded.

Ms. Lin put the knife back in the lunch bag and stashed it on a shelf behind her desk.

Now Sierra would have to go to French without eating anything. Maybe she could retrieve her oatmeal raisin cookies and gobble them on her way to class. But something made her think she'd better quit while she was ahead.

15

She was halfway to the door when Ms. Lin called out sharply, "Where do you think you're going, missy?"

Missy? Ms. Lin had never spoken to Sierra in that way.

"To French. I have French sixth period."

"You're not going anywhere." Ms. Lin pointed to the same row of chairs where Sierra had been sitting earlier. "Mr. Besser is out of the building right now, but I expect him back some time this afternoon."

This *afternoon?* Sierra couldn't miss French; they were having a quiz on irregular verbs. She didn't want to miss art. If she missed art, her pot might not be ready for the kiln by Friday, just two days away. And then there was the science lab where they'd be dissecting a worm. And, yes, dissecting it with a knife.

"Couldn't you tell Mr. Besser what happened? That it was all a mistake? I have a quiz in French and—"

"You'll just have to miss it."

"But . . . can I at least go to my locker to get my French book so I can study while I'm waiting?"

Ms. Lin shook her head.

Sierra felt her cheeks burning. She couldn't believe how unreasonable Ms. Lin was being when it was as completely obvious as anything in the world could be that an honor student like Sierra wouldn't bring a knife to school on purpose. Maybe Lexi and Em had been right. She should have just hidden the knife in her lunch bag.

Celeste had been the only one at the table who said nothing. Would Celeste have turned in the knife if she had been in Sierra's place? Or did she just want to see what would happen if Sierra did?

Tears pricked Sierra's eyes. She blinked them back and stared straight ahead. What if . . . ? No. She had clearly done the correct thing by giving the knife to Sandy. If only Mr. Besser would come in soon and straighten this out so that she could be back in French class before sixth period was over.

3

It was halfway through seventh period before Mr. Besser appeared, bustling into the outer office from the hallway. He was still in his overcoat and the fur hat that made him look like someone from a Russian movie. Another man was with him, a man Sierra hadn't seen before. Maybe someone's dad. But he didn't look like a dad.

"Ms. Lin," Mr. Besser began, "I'd like you to meet Elliot Granger. He's the new principal over at West Glen Middle School. He's here to check out some of the terrific programs we've put in place at our school."

His gaze fell on Sierra. "And some of our terrific students!" he added heartily, giving Sierra his usual big grin.

Sierra forced a smile as Ms. Lin and the other principal shook hands. Why, oh why, couldn't Mr. Besser have been alone? How could she talk to Mr. Besser and explain everything with that other principal there? Mr. Besser was busy now, too busy to deal with what was, after all, just a very small misunderstanding. But right now it didn't feel small to Sierra, not if it was making her miss a French quiz *and* pottery *and* maybe even a science lab.

Mr. Besser and his visitor turned to go into the inner office.

"Mr. Besser," Ms. Lin called after him. "I hate to disturb you, but something fairly urgent has come up."

Well, it certainly felt urgent to Sierra.

"A student brought a weapon to school today."

Sierra's breath caught in her chest.

Mr. Besser's eyes registered a flicker of irritation. He couldn't be pleased to have this news item blurted out in front of the visitor he was clearly trying to impress. Then he got his expression back under control.

Before Sierra could speak, he said smoothly, "Elliot, this will give you a chance to see how we operate here at Longwood. When I took over here, three years ago, discipline was . . . Well, the kindest way of putting it is lax. As a result, our best students were transferring out in droves to charter schools that took academics seriously and created a climate in which students actually came to school to learn."

Mr. Besser gestured to the banner above Sierra's head. "Every single student knows our core values now. Rules. Respect. Responsibility. Reliability. I can't say that every single student lives up to them, but at least now we all know what we're aiming for."

His genial smile fell again on Sierra. "In fact, I believe this young lady was one of our fine student leaders who sewed this banner for us. Isn't that right, Sierra?"

Sierra suddenly realized: *He doesn't get it.* Mr. Besser clearly had no idea that she was the student who had "brought a weapon to school today."

She had to tell him, but she didn't know how to interrupt.

"How *do* you handle a weapons incident?" Mr. Granger asked.

"We have a zero-tolerance policy for both weapons and drugs. No exceptions. No excuses. All our students know that."

But surely "No exceptions" didn't mean no exceptions even for an honor student who brought her mother's knife to school by mistake. Surely "No excuses" didn't mean no excuses even for a student leader who turned in the knife the minute she found it.

Mr. Granger gave an approving nod.

"Who was it?" Mr. Besser asked Ms. Lin. "Have you called his parents yet?"

He turned back to Mr. Granger. "And all our students know that zero tolerance doesn't mean a slap on the wrist, writing on the chalkboard a hundred times 'I will not bring a weapon to school,' or a three-day in-school suspension."

"So it means . . . ?"

"Expulsion. Mandatory expulsion. It wasn't Luke Bishop, was it?" Mr. Besser asked Ms. Lin.

"No." Ms. Lin looked at Sierra. "You tell him."

This couldn't be happening. There had to be some way to make it come out right—there had to be.

Sierra said, "It was me."

4

It was a mistake," Sierra said. How many times had she said those words already? How many more times would she have to say them? She was afraid she'd cry if she tried to explain the rest.

Ms. Lin finally helped her out: "She says the knife was in her mother's lunch, and the lunches got switched."

Sierra let herself glance at Mr. Besser. She had never seen him this way before, as if he had somehow stumbled into a blind trap. He was obviously stalling to give himself time to think about what to do next.

"Look," he finally said. "I can't deal with this now. Mr. Granger has given up his afternoon, taken time out of his busy schedule, to come meet with me. Ms. Lin, call Sierra's parents and explain what's happened. Tell them that they need to come and get her and that I'll meet with them first thing in the morning."

Sierra wanted to say, *But what about my science lab?*

She didn't.

Sierra wanted to ask, *But why do you have to have a meeting with my parents when this is obviously just a terrible mistake?*

She didn't.

Maybe the other principal would give some kind of chuckle, and it would become a friendly joke—a joke partly on Mr. Besser for just having said all that stuff about mandatory expulsion, with no exceptions ever, for weapons or drugs in his middle school. And partly on Sierra for having gotten herself caught up in such a ridiculous mess.

The two men disappeared into the inner office, and the door shut behind them.

"Should I try your father first, or your mother?" Ms. Lin asked Sierra.

"Can't I go to eighth period? For my science lab?"

For an answer, Ms. Lin picked up the receiver and poised her finger, ready to dial.

"My mother," Sierra said.

She gave Ms. Lin the number, and Ms. Lin made the call.

Sierra's mother didn't really work. Well, she thought she did, but the kind of things she did all day didn't seem like an actual job to Sierra. Her mother was trying to write plays. No one was paying her money to write them; she was just writing them because she wanted to. She took it seriously—she went to a playwriting group, and she entered playwriting contests. She had gotten an honorable mention in a contest last year. Sometimes, to make a little bit of money, she substituted in Sierra's former preschool. That's where her mother had gone today, with the wrong lunch bag.

Had her mother even noticed that she had taken Sierra's lunch? Had she thought to herself, *Wait, what about the knife?*

Apparently not.

Her mother didn't notice things like that.

Her father did.

Just as the dismissal bell rang, Sierra's mother came bursting into the office, coatless despite the January weather, her frizzy hair standing out from her head like a wild halo.

The first thing she did was gather Sierra into a hug, holding her so close that Sierra could feel her mother's heart throbbing.

"I'm sorry I couldn't come sooner," she told Sierra. "There was no one else to watch the children."

Sierra couldn't help herself. A gulping sob shook her shoulders. It had been too awful. Kept out of all her afternoon classes. The way Ms. Lin had called her "missy." That terrible trapped look in Mr. Besser's eyes as if he might really be ready to expel her—to *expel* her—for one tiny, infinitesimal moment of carelessness as she had grabbed her lunch off the kitchen counter.

Her mother held Sierra for a long moment. Then she turned to Ms. Lin. "We cannot wait until tomorrow morning to speak to Mr. Besser. I need to see him now."

"I'm afraid that's impossible," Ms. Lin said, making a big show of busying herself at her computer. "Mr. Besser is in a meeting."

"Where is his meeting?"

Ms. Lin didn't answer.

"He's in his office, isn't he? I'm sorry, Ms. Lin, but he is not sending this poor child home to worry about this ridiculousness all night long."

Sierra had never seen her mother so angry. Before Ms. Lin had time to leap up and block the door—if she would have done such a thing, which Sierra doubted, even on this bizarrely topsy-turvy day—Sierra's mother had pushed her way into the inner office.

"Stop," Ms. Lin called after her. "You can't just barge in there like that."

Sierra didn't follow after her mother. She couldn't bear to see the kindly, affectionate light gone from Mr. Besser's eyes when he looked at her. She lowered herself back down onto the hard plastic chair where she had already spent her long, miserable afternoon.

Two minutes later, her mother was back, eyes flaming, cheeks burning.

"Let's go," she told Sierra. Then she turned to Ms. Lin. "Sierra's father and I will see you tomorrow."

Even if Sierra's mother couldn't fix this hideous mess, her father could. Her father had to.

5

When Sierra turned on her cell phone in the car to check her messages, she had three texts.

Celeste: *Why weren't you in French?*

Lexi: *What did Sandy the lunch Nazi do to you?*

Em: *Call me.*

Sierra decided she would call her friends, not just text them, but waited until she was upstairs in her bedroom with the door closed.

She called Em first.

"What's going on?" Em asked.

Sierra could hardly bring herself to say it. "Ms. Lin and Mr. Besser? They're making a big deal about this."

"What kind of a big deal?"

"I don't know. Just a big deal. Like, they wouldn't let me go to any of my classes, and they called my mom to come get me. My dad's going to go ballistic when he finds out. Em, what will I do if they expel me?"

"Get real. They're not going to expel someone like

you," Em pointed out. "Not for something like this, whatever the rule says."

Sierra was lying on her bed, her beautiful four-poster bed with the old-fashioned blue-and-white fabric canopy like the ones in Colonial Williamsburg. Her cat, Cornflake, was lying there with her. It was hard to believe that anything too bad could happen when an overweight orange tabby was purring on her chest, one lazy paw stretched out across her shoulder.

"I know," she said, trying to sound confident. "It's just über-annoying. Now I have to make up the French quiz and the science lab, and it's, you know, one more thing."

"Colin asked me where you were in French class," Em said.

Sierra jerked up so abruptly that Cornflake jumped off her chest and settled himself nearby on the blue-patterned log cabin quilt.

"Did he really?"

"Uh-huh."

"What exactly did he say?"

"He said, 'Where's Sierra?'"

Sierra laughed. "How did he look when he said it?"

"Like he always looks. His voice was quiet—you know how it's almost whispery, sort of?"

Sierra did. His soft voice made him sound not wimpy, but soulful and poetic.

She felt embarrassed asking the next question, but she couldn't resist. "I mean, did he look worried?"

27

There was a silence: Sierra knew Em was carefully considering the question. Em never said anything that wasn't as accurate as she could make it.

"Not worried as much as puzzled. Because you were there for language arts and math this morning, and then you weren't there at French."

Sierra felt a twinge of disappointment. She didn't want Colin asking about her out of idle curiosity.

"What did you tell him?"

"I just said you had some stuff you had to do in the office."

"Then what did he say?"

"He said, 'But she's missing a quiz.'"

That sounded more like being worried than being puzzled. She could hear him saying it, too. *But she's missing a quiz.* Colin had definitely been concerned, concerned about *her.*

Sierra called Lexi next.

"You should have just kept the stupid knife in the lunch bag," Lexi moaned. "Em told you, and I thought so, too. Then none of this would have happened."

"Well, you were right, I guess."

"Lin is a bitch," Lexi said.

A few hours ago, Sierra would have said, *Oh, she's not so bad.* And "bitch" was such an awful, ugly word. But right now it seemed pretty accurate.

"You know what she did to me once?" Lexi went on. "I was running down the hall by the front office—not

28

completely running, but going pretty fast. And she made me stop. Okay, I can see making me stop. But then she said, 'Now go back to the library, and let me see you walk down the hall like a young lady.' It was so demeaning. Like I was two. And the bell rang, and she still kept watching me to see if I was walking slowly enough to please her, and I was late for pre-algebra."

"She called me 'missy,'" Sierra confessed.

"I hate her," Lexi said.

"I hate her, too."

Sierra didn't feel like calling Celeste. Celeste's silence at the lunch table had felt so superior, even smug. But if Sierra didn't get back to Celeste, Celeste would just keep texting.

"You weren't in French," Celeste said as soon as she answered her phone. "And I heard you weren't in art or science either."

"Well, you know Ms. Lin." Sierra tried to put the best face on it. "She's such a stickler for rules. She just has this huge thing about them, so I had to sit there forever to wait for Mr. Besser, and then I couldn't really talk to him anyway."

"Are they going to let you go to school tomorrow?"

The question punched Sierra like a fist in the stomach. What if she didn't get to go to class tomorrow, or the next day, or the day after that? What if she really did get expelled and never returned to any of her classes ever again?

She couldn't let herself think that way.

"Of course!"

"Then why wouldn't they let you go to class this afternoon?"

"Because Ms. Lin's crazy." Sierra still couldn't bring herself to use Lexi's word. "And Mr. Besser was busy in a meeting with this other principal who was doing a tour of our school to get ideas for his school."

"Sierra," Celeste said as if she were a grownup trying to get a child's attention. "Don't you get it? If anyone brings a knife to school, *for whatever reason*, they get expelled. You could get *expelled* for this."

Sierra's chest tightened. What if Em was wrong and Celeste was right?

"Look," Sierra snapped. "They're not going to expel someone for a total and complete mistake! Anyway, I've got to go. I have a ton of homework."

"Okay," Celeste said mildly. But then she asked, "So you'll be at choir?"

Sierra *wasn't* going to be at choir tomorrow morning. During the before-school choir practice, she was going to be in a conference with Mr. Besser and her parents. But she couldn't bear to say that to Celeste.

"Sure," Sierra said with false bravado. "See you then."

Maybe she'd be done with the meeting in time to get to choir after all.

Or maybe she'd never be allowed to go to a choir practice ever again.

She pulled Cornflake close to her after she hung up the phone, wanting the comfort of the cat's warm, plump body cuddled against her, but Cornflake struggled out of Sierra's embrace and stalked away.

6

Sierra had thought her dad might come home early—
she knew her mother had called him at the office—but
he stayed at work even later than usual, so Sierra and her
mother had dinner alone. She heard his car pulling into
the garage at half past eight and hurried downstairs to
see him.

Before he even took off his coat he said, "Sorry I'm
late. We're just two days away from trial on the Wilson
case. I had to take care of some things tonight in order to
clear my calendar for tomorrow morning so that I can go
into school with you and your mother and see what the
hell is going on there."

"I saved you some taco casserole," Sierra's mother
told him.

He waved her away. "We had dinner delivered at the
office. Sierra, honey, you tell me everything that happened. Okay? Every single thing."

Sierra's mom hung his coat for him in the hall closet as he settled himself at the kitchen table and opened his laptop to take notes.

Sierra couldn't decide if she felt relieved or even more frightened. Her dad was an attorney, one of the best in the city, or at least that's what everybody always told her, including her dad himself. But the grim set of his jaw and the way he drew his eyebrows together made him look as if he was readying himself for a battle, and not a little battle, either.

Sierra told him how she had found the ham sandwich and then realized she had the wrong lunch. She told him how she had spilled out the entire contents of the lunch bag and seen the knife.

He stopped her. "You should have called me right then. That's what you have a cell phone for. Not to text your friends all night long, but to call us in case of an emergency."

Sierra felt as if she were facing her father in the court-room, waiting to see if he was going to stop her for cross-examination after every single sentence.

"We're not allowed to use cell phones at school," she explained. "That's the rule."

"None of this would have happened if you'd called me first."

Sierra was curious now. "What would you have told me to do?"

"I'd have told you to put the fool thing away before anyone else saw it, and I'd have sent your mother over to school to switch lunches with you immediately."

"I couldn't have left work like that," Sierra's mother put in. "Not in the middle of lunch. It's our busiest time of the day. As it was, I couldn't even get away until almost three."

"So this is what we ended up with instead? Hell, I'd have left my meeting and hightailed it over to your school myself. Okay. Go on. What happened next?"

"Well, I took the knife to Sandy—she's the lunch lady—and she went with me to the office, and then we gave it to Ms. Lin—she's the school secretary."

Her father interrupted her again. "And neither of those women had the sense to have you call your parents to come get the knife right away, before all this got blown out of proportion? A murderer gets to make a phone call, but a seventh grader who took the wrong lunch to school by mistake isn't instructed about her legal rights?"

He was typing furiously on his computer as he spoke.

Sierra told him about Mr. Besser's arrival in the office with the other principal and the conversation the two men had had about Longwood's zero-tolerance policy for weapons and drugs.

Her father stopped typing.

"Oh, this is bad."

Sierra's heart clogged her throat. "It is?"

"I know Besser. My office did some work for his wife's

business years ago. He's a decent enough guy. A bit in love with himself, as principals tend to be, a man surrounded all day by a bunch of women, spending most of his time bossing around short people." Her dad gave a mirthless chuckle.

Sierra would have expected her father to want her to have respect for school principals in general, and her school principal in particular. This was the first time she had ever heard him talk about Mr. Besser in this way. But it was also the first time Mr. Besser had ever done anything to upset him.

Her father continued: "But, as I said, he's decent and he means well, and I give him credit for turning the school around, reclaiming it from the druggie kids and their loser parents, and making it a place where smart kids get the education they deserve."

Sierra's dad raked his hand through his thick silver hair. His hair had turned completely gray before he was forty.

"But now he can't back down, don't you see? Because the other guy has heard him do all his grandstanding. Now he can't do what any reasonable person with half a brain and half a conscience would do and forget all about this. Because he's painted himself into a corner."

"The other principal seemed pretty nice," Sierra said timidly.

"Nice has nothing to do with it."

Sierra remembered that trapped look on Mr. Besser's

face. Now she saw that same look on her father's face, too.

"Next time . . ." her father said. "Next time anything like this happens, ever, you call me. I don't care what rules there are about cell phones. You call me."

"Sierra," her mother said. She had been so quiet during the last few minutes that Sierra had almost forgotten she was still there. "Why *didn't* you put the knife back in the bag right away? Why did you give it to Sandy?"

Sierra wasn't sure she even remembered. It all seemed to have happened so long ago.

"I just thought I was supposed to turn it in," she said finally. "I just thought it was the right thing to do."

7

The bell for the start of first period was at 8:05. Sierra and her parents were in the school office, waiting for Mr. Besser's arrival, at 7:15.

"We want all this crap taken care of so that you can be in your seat when your first class begins," Sierra's father had told her as he had backed the car, too fast, out of the driveway. Sierra hoped it would all be taken care of even sooner than that: in time for her to go to most of choir practice.

The Longwood Middle School halls were empty at that hour except for a few teachers hurrying to their rooms to prepare their lesson plans for the day. No students were allowed in the building until 7:45 unless they were there for a before-school extracurricular activity, like the Octave. Or there, as Sierra was, with their parents.

Ms. Lin and Mrs. Saunders were already at their desks when Sierra and her parents came in.

Mrs. Saunders gave them a worried-looking smile as Ms. Lin greeted them.

"Good morning! There's a coatrack over there if you want to leave your coats. And may I get you anything while you wait? Coffee? Tea?"

Ms. Lin seemed to have had a personality transplant overnight. Sierra suspected it was occasioned by the presence of her father, Gerald Edward Shepard, Esquire, attorney-at-law.

"Thanks, but we're fine," her dad said.

Sierra had a feeling her mother might have accepted the offer of tea if her father hadn't spoken first. Her mother loved tea, and if they were all sipping tea together, maybe it would seem more like a friendly social visit. Her father removed his coat, and Sierra's mother shrugged off her jacket; her father hung them both up on the coatrack. Sierra kept hers on. She was cold, more from fear than from the frigid January morning.

She wondered if her dad would yell at Ms. Lin, call her grossly incompetent to her face, demand an explanation for why Sierra hadn't been directed to make a phone call to her parents.

He didn't. He just sat reading the copy of *The Wall Street Journal* that he had brought with him. Sierra remembered he had once said that he didn't "waste energy on flunkies."

Neither Sierra nor her mother had brought anything

to read. Her mother took Sierra's hand and rubbed her thumb gently against Sierra's wrist.

The office door opened, and Mr. Besser came in wearing the same big coat and fur hat he had worn yesterday.

"Hello, Gerald!" he greeted Sierra's dad, who stood up to accept his handshake.

Her dad was taller than Mr. Besser, but by barely an inch.

As he shrugged off his coat and removed his hat, Mr. Besser turned toward Sierra's mom. "Hello, Angie."

Neither Mr. Besser nor Sierra's mother gave any sign of acknowledging that they had spoken unpleasant words to each other just yesterday.

"And Sierra." Mr. Besser hung up his coat and hat; he smiled at Sierra without meeting her eyes. "Well, come on into my office. Can Ms. Lin get you some coffee? Tea?"

Sierra's father shook his head, less graciously than he had before, as if to say, *Let's cut the crap.*

Mr. Besser replaced his welcoming smile with a look of sad seriousness.

Sierra followed her parents into the inner sanctum and took one of the chairs facing Mr. Besser's desk. He probably had three chairs for his guests because he so often met with a problem student and the student's parents.

Luke Bishop must have sat there with his parents. Now Sierra Shepard was sitting there with hers.

Sierra's father spoke first.

"We're here to demand an apology for the unconscionable and illegal way in which your staff treated our daughter yesterday. She is to receive a full apology from you and your secretary. She is to receive an excused absence in the three classes she was wrongly forced to miss."

Sierra's father always said that the best defense was a good offense.

"Mr. Shepard," Mr. Besser began. Apparently they were no longer on a chummy, first-name basis. "Our school has a policy—an ironclad policy, I might say—that prohibits any weapons or any drugs on school grounds for any reason. For any reason whatsoever. Indeed, the existence of that policy is one of the main reasons that parents choose to enroll their students here. All students who enroll here, and all parents who enroll their children here, know that policy and sign a form stating that they are fully aware of what that policy entails. You and Mrs. Shepard signed the policy; we have your form on file."

"But that policy needs to be administered with a small dose of common sense," Sierra's father interrupted.

"Please let me finish."

Sierra's mother took Sierra's hand again.

"Do I think that Sierra brought that knife to school on purpose?" Mr. Besser said, speaking slowly as if to convey to Sierra's dad his unwillingness to be rushed. "No. Do I think she acted appropriately in turning it in? Yes. Do I think that what has happened here is unfortunate? Absolutely. But does that mean that I can make an exception in her case? No."

Sierra's mother was rubbing the side of Sierra's hand so hard that it felt as if she might wear a hole in the skin.

"A zero-tolerance policy has risks that some innocent student, like your daughter, will be an unintended victim of the policy. I would be the first to say how distressing this is, for all of us. But it's even more distressing when a student gets stabbed with a knife, or slashed with a switchblade, or shot with a handgun. Zero-tolerance policies exist to make sure that these far worse tragedies don't happen."

Mr. Besser seemed to have finished his speech. Now it was Sierra's father's turn.

"You cannot sit there with a straight face and tell me that you could possibly believe that you have made this school safer in any way whatsoever by taking action against an honor student who brought the wrong lunch to school by mistake and took immediate steps to address the situation."

Mr. Besser raised his hands, palms up, as if to signify his helplessness in the face of what had to be. "We have a *zero-tolerance* policy regarding weapons and drugs here at Longwood Middle School. And, let me remind you, we weren't the ones who made this regrettable mistake. It was your daughter's mistake."

"It was my mistake," Sierra's mother inserted. "I'm the one who took the wrong lunch and left mine on the table."

"It was your *family*'s mistake," Mr. Besser corrected.

The two men locked gazes. It seemed to Sierra that her fate would be decided by which man looked away first. She knew it wouldn't be her father. Never in his life had he looked away first.

Sure enough, Mr. Besser glanced down at his desk, as if some important paper there demanded his sudden attention.

"But—" Sierra's mother spoke, her voice shaking, not with yesterday's anger but with audible agitation. "What does this mean for *Sierra*?"

"Of course, the school district will observe all due-process requirements," Mr. Besser said smoothly. "There will be a hearing next Friday, a week from tomorrow, with the superintendent present, and myself as well. Your family is entitled to hire legal representation to accompany you to that meeting if you choose to do so."

"But what's going to *happen* to Sierra?" her mother persisted, despite her father's hand laid warningly on her arm.

"The hearing will be for expulsion," Mr. Besser said.

Sierra's heart swelled up in her chest, blocking her throat, blocking the supply of air to her lungs.

"And in the meantime?" Sierra's mother continued. "Can she still go to her classes? And to her other activities, like Leadership Club and the Octave?"

"I regret, no. She'll report to school each day for in-school suspension."

"And if someone *is* expelled, what happens then? Where do they—"

"Angie." Sierra's father cut her off, obviously unwilling to allow any speculation whatsoever about what would happen if Mr. Besser really succeeded in having Sierra expelled.

"Students who have been expelled continue to have a right to a free public education," Mr. Besser replied, as if Sierra's father hadn't spoken. "The district maintains an alternative-school option for such students."

Sierra's dad stood up. Mr. Besser stood up, too.

"That is ridiculous," Sierra's father said, his voice holding steady despite the vein popping in his jaw. "Sierra is not going to be expelled, and she is not going to serve an in-school suspension. Until this matter is resolved, Sierra is coming home with us. She isn't going to sit here for more than a week like a juvenile delinquent—like a common criminal."

"I'm afraid that under state truancy law, parents do not have the option to refuse to let their children serve an in-school suspension," Mr. Besser replied. "I'd advise you and your wife to comply with the law on this matter."

Sierra wasn't sure exactly what Mr. Besser meant. But she could read on her father's face that the principal had scored a point.

"I have some advice for you, too, Tom," her father said. "I'd suggest that you hire yourself a very, very good lawyer."

He turned and walked out of Mr. Besser's office.

"Oh, honey," her mother said, pulling Sierra into another fierce hug.

"So I have to stay here?" Sierra asked in a choked whisper.

"Just until your father can get this sorted out. But he will. You know he will."

"Mrs. Shepard, Sierra, I truly am sorry," Mr. Besser said. He came around from his side of the desk to escort them to the door.

"I truly am sorry," he repeated.

His eyes, as they fell on Sierra, glistened with something suspiciously like tears.

8

Ms. Lin led Sierra down a short hallway off the back of the front office to a small room that contained only a conference table surrounded by half a dozen chairs. Sierra had never known this room existed.

No one else was there yet. It was still ten minutes before the first bell, and bad kids weren't the kind to show up bright and early for their in-school suspension.

"You may study or read," Ms. Lin told Sierra. "When the others arrive, you may talk quietly among yourselves. No electronic devices are permitted—no iPods, cell phones, Game Boys."

As if Sierra had ever played a video game in her life.

"If you need to use the restroom, come tell me and I'll give you a pass."

Ms. Lin avoided making eye contact with Sierra as she spoke. Sierra hoped it was because, down deep, Ms. Lin was ashamed of herself for treating her this way.

After Ms. Lin left, Sierra pressed her forehead down on the table, feeling the coolness of the wood veneer surface against her face.

She couldn't sit here all day, every day, for a whole week.

But after a few minutes she made herself take the books out of her backpack and set them neatly on the table in front of her. At least she could work on her Mayan culture report for social studies. Her father wasn't going to let her be expelled. It would be silly to sit paralyzed, doing nothing, and fall even further behind in everything.

Another girl appeared, someone Sierra had never seen before—an eighth grader? Then five minutes after the bell, the boy who had been fighting with Luke; and then five minutes later, Luke himself.

Sierra Shepard was now officially serving an in-school suspension with Luke Bishop.

The first two had taken no notice of Sierra, which was fine with her. She had barely glanced up as they entered. But Luke did a double take when he saw her.

"Whoa," he said. "What is Little Miss Shep-turd doing here?"

Sierra didn't answer, pretending to be too absorbed in copying notes from her library book onto index cards.

"Don't tell me. You're doing research for your new school project that is going to help kids like me, so you can write it up for your application for the Nobel Peace Prize."

He plopped himself down in the chair next to her and, from his pocket, produced his Game Boy.

"I thought we weren't allowed to use electronic devices," Sierra said before she could stop herself.

"Ooh!" Luke said. "And if I got caught with a Game Boy, I might get in trouble."

"They could extend your suspension," Sierra pointed out, even though she had no intention of being drawn into a prolonged conversation with Luke.

"Ooh!" he said again. "That would be awful! I'd miss class!"

Sierra copied another fact about the Mayans onto a note card. Luke leaned over to see what she had written.

"You're kidding!" He mimed surprise. "There is a Mayan temple called Chichén Itzá? What kind of name is that for a temple? *Chicken?*" He gave some loud chicken clucks while making chicken motions with his arms.

"I can't take notes if you keep talking," Sierra told him.

Not to mention clucking.

Luke gestured toward the clock that hung on the far wall, a wall otherwise bare of decoration except for a hand-lettered poster with the school values: RULES RESPECT RESPONSIBILITY RELIABILITY. The poster was nowhere near as attractive as the banner in the front office, which seemed sort of backward to Sierra. The kids in the suspension room were the ones who really needed to learn to appreciate that message.

"We're here until three-ten. Seven hours. I don't think you're exactly in a big time crunch. So, really, why are you here?" Luke pressed.

"It's none of your business." Sierra wondered how Luke would react if she did tell him. Would he be indignant on her behalf? Or gleeful to see the tables turned for once?

"Tiff, Mitch, what do you think she did? Tiffany used inappropriate language to Lintbag when Lintbag told her to take off her baseball cap. Mitch and I were fighting, but we've made it up now, right, Mitch?"

Mitch scowled at Luke and said nothing.

"Tiff, you guess first. What did Little Miss Shep-turd do that got her put in here with us?"

Tiffany studied Sierra. Tiffany's hair was black—dyed? And she had not only a pierced eyebrow but a pierced nose, too. It was strange that the school rules prohibited baseball caps but permitted nose rings.

"What do I care?" Tiffany finally said.

"Mitch?"

"Someone jumped her when she was doing nothing, and then *she* got in trouble for fighting."

"Then where's the other kid?"

Mitch shrugged. "In the hospital getting stitches on her face."

"Warm or cold?" Luke asked Sierra.

Well, it was sort of warm, in that she was in trouble even though she hadn't done a single thing that was wrong, and it was all completely unfair. But Sierra would never hit someone.

Still: "Warm, I guess."

"You were in a *fight?*"

"No! But I'm here for a reason that's completely unfair. Like being here for fighting if someone else started the fight—that would be completely unfair."

"Yeah," Mitch said, glaring again at Luke.

"Come on, Tiff, take a guess," Luke urged.

"Why don't *you* take a guess?" Tiff had started painting her fingernails. She was squinting down at them with fierce concentration.

"Okay." Luke turned toward Sierra. "You cheated on a test. And you think it's unfair that you got caught because you really need an A on the test so that you can get into a special talented and gifted summer camp, which you need to put on your application when you apply to Princeton someday. Warm or cold?"

"Cold! I would never cheat. And if I did, and I got caught, I couldn't say it was unfair, because it would be totally fair."

"I give up. Tiffany, help!"

"You were hooking up in the stairwell with someone." Tiffany extended the fingers of her left hand and studied them intently.

"No!" Sierra felt her cheeks flaming. The closest she had come to kissing a boy was imagining kissing Colin, wondering if his lips would be as soft as his voice.

At this rate, it would be better just to tell them.

"Okay, I brought my mother's lunch to school. By mistake. We both have the same lunch bag. And she had an apple, and a knife for cutting it. I turned in the knife right away. I gave it to Sandy, and now . . ."

Sierra's voice was trembling. It was impossible that this thing had happened to her not even twenty-four hours ago.

Luke gave a low whistle.

"You're screwed," he said.

Sierra thought his look had some pity in it. Mitch had also winced with painful understanding. Tiffany had started in on the fingers of her other hand.

"No, I'm not," Sierra said. "My father is an attorney. Like a really big-time attorney, and he's going to get it all straightened out. He is."

"And you think *I'm* going to get in trouble for using my Game Boy?" was all Luke said.

9

The morning lasted forever. Every time the bell rang for the end of another period, Sierra thought about another class she had missed, more work that she would have to make up. The boys played games on their Game Boys; Tiffany sat doing absolutely nothing except thinking her own thoughts. Sierra dutifully copied out note card after note card, but even the most perfect straight-A student would find research boring after almost three hours.

When the bell rang for the start of 4A, Ms. Lin appeared for the third or fourth time in the room. Each time, the Game Boys vanished the instant her clicking heels sounded down the hall.

"If you brought your lunch, you may eat it now," Ms. Lin said. "If not, Mrs. Saunders will take you to the cafeteria, where you will buy your lunch. You will return with your tray and eat here in the suspension room."

Sierra had brought money to buy her lunch; she had

decided that morning that she never wanted to take the risk of bringing a lunch from home ever again. But now the shame of being led to the cafeteria with an escort—a prison guard—was unbearable.

"I'm not hungry," Sierra said.

Ms. Lin pursed her lips. "Suit yourself. But if you don't go now, you can't go later."

Luke and Mitch followed Ms. Lin out of the room. Tiffany pulled a crumpled-looking paper bag from her backpack. In it was a sandwich, a can of soda, a bag of chips, and a bag of store-bought chocolate-chip cookies.

"Want some?"

Tiffany shoved her bag of chips toward Sierra.

"Sure. I mean, thanks."

Sierra took a few chips from the bag.

Wordlessly, Tiffany pushed her bag of cookies toward Sierra as well. Sierra took one of those, too.

"Thanks," Sierra said again.

She couldn't think what else to say. She knew she wasn't supposed to ask if the nose ring hurt. Or if it was awkward blowing your nose with a ring in the way.

"I think it was gutsy, what you said to Ms. Lin," Sierra finally said.

"You don't even know what I said."

"Luke said you said *something*. Something bad enough to get you suspended."

"Just for one day. And it wasn't like a big, brave, heroic moment. I was pissed off."

"I don't see why you can't wear a baseball cap if you want to."

Especially if they let you wear a nose ring.

Tiffany shrugged. "It's their school. I guess they can make whatever rules they want."

"It's not their school. The school belongs to all of us."

"It doesn't belong to me."

The boys returned, carrying their trays. The hot lunch was pizza, cut in rectangular slabs, with a small paper cup filled with cooked green beans and another small paper cup filled with applesauce.

Sierra should have swallowed her pride and gotten the school lunch. It had been horrible having to go without lunch yesterday, and now here she was, missing lunch again. Three potato chips and one cookie hardly counted as a meal.

"Aren't you going to eat anything?" Luke asked her.

"It's too late now. Ms. Lin said so."

"You can have my green beans. I don't want them, but it's a law or something that they have to give them to you anyway, so the lunch will count as nutritious. I'm just going to throw them away."

"You can have my green beans, too," Mitch said. "And my applesauce."

Sierra accepted both offers gratefully.

Her mother always said that everything happened for a reason. Maybe the reason Sierra had gotten a completely unfair in-school suspension was so she could learn that the bad kids weren't as bad as she had thought they were, that they were actually pretty nice.

If so, she had learned that lesson by noon on the first day.

I get it, Sierra silently told the universe as she chewed on Mitch's rubbery, cold green beans. *I really do. Can I go back to class now?*

But the universe didn't bother to reply.

There was no window in the suspension room. Rain, sleet, snow could fall for hours, and it would make no difference to the unchanging, boring fate of the prisoners within.

When the closing bell finally sounded, Sierra shouldered her backpack and headed out to the front hall. Maybe Em or Lexi would be looking for her before they went to the home basketball game. Maybe even Colin. He was the kind of boy who noticed when things weren't right. He might have figured out where she was and be loitering inconspicuously by the front office, just in case.

"Darling!"

It was her mother, her face pale with worry. Sierra let herself be enfolded in her mother's hug.

"Are you okay?" her mother asked anxiously. "I thought about you every minute all day long. I've been waiting here for the last half hour."

"I'm okay. Can we go now?"

"Of course. I have the car right outside. There are a

whole bunch of news vans lined up for something—did you hear of anything going on? Anyway, I parked in the no-parking zone."

Her mother gave a forced chuckle. Oh, the Shepards were becoming daring. That rebellious, rule-defying mother-daughter pair!

Sierra stayed within her mother's encircling arm as they walked outside into the biting January air.

In the asphalt circle in front of the school she saw not one, not two, but three panel vans with big dish antennas on top. On the side of the closest one Sierra could read the words "9NEWS" with the familiar station logo. Something big indeed must have happened at school today while she was locked away in her windowless room.

Then: "There she is!" she heard someone yell from the cluster of reporters and cameramen standing together by the vans.

"There's Sierra Shepard!"

10

The TV cameras drew closer as Sierra and her mother walked together down the front steps of the school. When they reached the sidewalk, a woman with perfectly coiffed blond hair, every strand welded into place by industrial-strength hair spray, was by Sierra's side, pointing a microphone toward her.

"Sierra," the woman said pleasantly. "Sierra Shepard, right? We're here to get your side of the story. Tell us what happened."

Sierra looked over at her mother. Was she supposed to answer or not? She remembered once seeing someone on the news, a man in a business suit, striding past a long row of reporters and cameras, holding up a newspaper to shield his face. Besides, how did the blond reporter and the cameraman *know*?

"Oh my God," her mother said in a low voice. "Your father said he was going to try to get some media attention for you, but I have to admit, I didn't expect . . . this." She sighed. "Go ahead and talk to them, sweetie."

"You brought the wrong lunch to school," the reporter prompted her.

"Um—I brought my mother's lunch, instead of mine, because we have the same lunch bag. I mean, our lunch bags look the same, and there was a little knife in it to cut an apple, and I gave it to the lunch lady right away, because I know we're not supposed to have knives at school."

"You turned it in the second you saw it?" the woman asked, even though that was exactly what Sierra had already said. "The instant you realized the mistake?"

"Yes."

Now another reporter was there, a man in a dark suit and a red tie, accompanied by his cameraman, too. The dark-suited reporter thrust his microphone close to her face.

"Have you ever been in trouble before, Sierra? Any previous suspensions? Detentions?"

"No, I'm in Leadership Club and—"

"What's the lowest grade you've ever received?"

"I got a B once, last year, third quarter, in earth science."

"You got a B *once*," he repeated. "Do you think Longwood Middle School's handling of this incident has been fair to you, Sierra?"

Even after everything that had happened, Sierra still felt disloyal criticizing Mr. Besser in public. He'd be angry at her; he wouldn't like her anymore. But she had to speak up for herself.

"No," she said. "I think it was unfair. It's completely unfair."

"Why?"

"Because it was a mistake, and I turned it in right away. I tried to do the right thing!" Sierra felt her voice start to wobble.

A third reporter, crowding close with his microphone, interrupted. "So you don't think you should be *expelled*"—he emphasized the word carefully—"just for trying to do the right thing?"

Now Sierra's eyes were filling with tears. Blinking hard, she turned away, knowing that the cameras were still trained on her, capturing every expression, including the shaking of her slumped shoulders.

"Are you Sierra's mother?" she heard the blond reporter ask.

Sierra slipped away and dropped down onto a large flat rock by the side of the school entrance, while her mother answered more questions.

"Hey."

She heard a soft voice. A soft male voice.

It was Colin.

"Celeste told me that you're suspended."

Sierra nodded. She could imagine Celeste bustling

about, pleased to be the first one to inform everybody, not that Celeste could have had any way of knowing for sure. But Celeste would have noticed that Sierra was absent all day and drawn her own conclusions, pleased to have been proven right yet again.

Didn't you know? Sierra's going to be expelled.

Standing while she was sitting, Colin looked taller than he actually was. The slight breeze, which had probably made Sierra look all windblown for the TV cameras, now lifted Colin's brown bangs off his face. Even though it was cold, he was wearing a hoodie, not a jacket.

"I think that's really unfair," he said.

It wasn't worth all this hideousness to have Colin Beauvoir gazing down at her with sympathetic, troubled eyes. But almost.

"I do, too."

"What's going to happen? Do you think they'll really expel you?"

"My dad's going to try to fix it."

She pointed to the panel vans for the three news stations. "I just talked to some reporters. For the TV news."

"Wow. I never knew anyone who was on TV before."

"Well, you never knew any big-time criminals before."

There. She had even made a joke about it.

"I'll be sure to watch the news tonight," Colin said.

Sierra hoped her hair wouldn't look too awful. She should have asked for time to comb it first. Plus, people said the camera put on ten pounds of weight. She'd look dumpy and fat, red-faced and ready to cry under her wind-mussed hair.

"You don't have to watch it."

It was a dumb thing to say: of course he didn't have to.

"It'll be cool if you're on TV." Colin smiled at her.

If his hands hadn't been jammed in his hoodie pockets, maybe they'd have been trembling in that poetic way she loved so much.

"Well, see you," Colin said.

If only she could be back in class tomorrow, sitting next to him.

"See you," she echoed.

When Sierra and her mother got home, there were seven calls on the answering machine from different newspapers all around the state, from the Associated Press, even from *The New York Times*. Each reporter left a cell phone number, asking Sierra to call back as soon as possible, any time; however late it was didn't matter.

"Your father," Sierra's mother said, "has been busy."

"Do I have to call them? All of them?"

Her mother nodded. "I know your father wants you to."

"What should I say?"

"Just what you've been saying. Keep telling the truth, that it was all a mistake, and that you turned in the knife the instant you found it. But first let me make you a snack. You must be hungry. What did you have for lunch?"

Sierra thought of Tiffany's potato chips and cookie, the boys' small paper cups of green beans and applesauce.

"I'm starving."

"I'll make you a grilled cheese sandwich. Would you like that? And some tomato soup? Go sit down and relax in the family room, and I'll bring it to you."

Sierra curled up on the couch and pulled an afghan over her legs. Cornflake came meowing; she patted the blanket, and he jumped up on her lap and began purring.

Idly, Sierra picked up the remote and clicked on the TV. It was set to CNN, her father's favorite channel.

At the bottom of the screen, the news banner scrolled by. COLORADO HONOR STUDENT FACING EXPULSION FOR BRINGING THE WRONG LUNCH TO SCHOOL.

Sierra stared at the TV.

11

By four-thirty, Sierra had talked to six reporters; she had left a message for the seventh, but he hadn't called her back yet. Each time she told the reporter the exact same story in almost the exact same words. By the sixth time, it had all begun to feel like just that, a *story*: something that had happened to somebody else, and not to her at all. She no longer felt her heart jam itself up against her ribs when she heard the question "Do you think you're going to be *expelled*?" Instead, she just answered "No."

There was no way that she, Sierra Shepard, was really going to be expelled from Longwood Middle School forever for one teensy, tiny, innocent mistake.

Each time she said it, she believed it more.

When she checked her phone, she saw she had tons of texts from Celeste, Lexi, and Em. She was too drained to call anyone now. Let them worry about her for a while, her friends who had been allowed to sit in class all day working toward their good grades while she was in prison—with Luke Bishop!—eating the cold green beans that Luke would otherwise have thrown away.

The doorbell rang.

For a fleeting moment Sierra wondered if it could be Mr. Besser, come to apologize, come to tell her he had changed his mind and her suspension was over. The same reporters had probably called him, too; maybe by the time he had repeated his defense of his zero-tolerance policy a dozen times it had started to sound as lame to him as it would to the entire rest of the universe.

Sierra's mother answered the door. From upstairs, Sierra heard her say, "Girls! Come on in!"

Celeste was the first to burst through the door into Sierra's room, with Lexi and Em right behind her. Cornflake leaped off Sierra's pillow and darted under the bed.

"We left, like, a hundred messages!" Celeste's tone was accusing.

"I was on the phone," Sierra explained as the girls plopped themselves down on Sierra's bed beneath her ruffled canopy. Sierra leaned back against the headboard. "To reporters. To six different reporters. I told Em my dad would go ballistic over this."

"Like, newspaper reporters?" Lexi asked.

"The *Denver Post*. The Associated Press. *The New York Times*."

As the names tripped so casually from her tongue,

Sierra for the first time felt impressed with herself, in a way that she hadn't felt when she had talked before to Colin. "And TV. Three local news stations were there after school, with huge cameras and everything. Oh, and I saw something about me on the thingie on the bottom of the screen on CNN."

She glanced over at Celeste, wondering if the pity in Celeste's eyes would turn to something more like amazement, even envy. Sierra's father liked to quote some artist—the one who had painted all those pictures of Campbell Soup cans—who said that everybody got to be famous for fifteen minutes. Maybe this was her fifteen minutes of fame right now. But she wished she could have been famous for something else, for a prize she had won, for something brilliant and wonderful that she had done.

"CNN?" Lexi asked. "Like, national TV?"

"Uh-huh."

"Holy moly." Lexi's eyes were gratifyingly huge. "I wonder if they came into the cafeteria and interviewed Sandy and she had to get off her stool. Or maybe they filmed her sitting on her stool."

Em and Celeste laughed, and Sierra let herself laugh, too.

"Or Ms. Lin. Maybe they had a hidden camera and filmed her being the bitch she is, and now the whole world will see. And Besser—that bow tie he always wears? Maybe they asked him why he seems to think it's cool to wear a bow tie when it's the least cool thing ever."

"Sometimes they film stuff for TV, but then it doesn't end up being on TV," Celeste said, stretching herself out full-length on Sierra's bed. "Like, something more important happens. A car wreck. Or a murder. I mean, I don't think someone getting suspended is as big as a murder." She paused. "You *were* suspended, right? That's why you weren't in class all day?"

Isn't that what you've already been telling everybody? Including Colin?

Sierra nodded.

"And are you really going to be expelled?" Celeste asked. She sounded as if she'd just as soon have Sierra expelled so that she could claim to have been the first to see it coming.

"Well, they have to have a hearing," Sierra said.

"They're not going to expel her," Lexi shot back, sitting bolt upright and hugging one of Sierra's pillows to her chest. "Not when it's on TV."

"Why not?" Celeste asked. "Why would that make any difference?"

"It would make Besser look so bad!" Lexi retorted. "Like the jerk to end all jerks! It's called bad publicity. As in terrible publicity."

Em hadn't said anything yet; she was busy coaxing Cornflake to reappear from under the bed and position himself on her lap.

"Em?" Sierra asked her, once Celeste had gotten up to go to the bathroom; Sierra could never talk as freely in front of Celeste. "What do you really think is going to happen to me?"

"I don't think they can expel you, not when it was all just a big mistake. It's horrible enough that they suspended you. Was it awful? Sitting in suspension?"

"It wasn't too bad." She had to say it. "Colin was waiting for me afterward."

Well, not really waiting for her. But sort of waiting. He might have been waiting. Her five minutes with Colin had been the only good part of a hideous day.

"He *does* like you!" Em said. "What exactly did he say?"

Sierra was grateful that Celeste was still out of the room.

"He said he was going to watch me on TV. He saw all the reporters filming me."

"So he'll be sitting in his house, and he'll turn on the TV, and he'll sit there gazing at you." Em gave a little imitation of what was supposed to be Colin's lovesick sigh.

"There's no way you can be expelled once you're on TV," Lexi repeated. "Once you're so famous, famous all over the country. Maybe even the world."

"You guys," Sierra said.

She was glad Em and Lexi had come over, even though she could have done without Celeste. Thank goodness Celeste hadn't heard her gushing about her crush on Colin.

But she would have been gladder if it had been Mr. Besser at the door, coming to put an end to this mess and to make everything all right again.

12

Sierra's father called to say that he wouldn't be home until late because of the Wilson trial tomorrow. Celeste and Lexi had to go home, but Em stayed to watch the six o'clock local news with Sierra and her mom.

They turned the TV in the family room to Channel 9. Sierra's mother leaned forward from her spot on the ottoman; the two girls sat side by side on the floor, legs outstretched, backs against the couch.

"Maybe it won't be on," Sierra said, echoing Celeste's words. "Maybe there'll be a murder or a car wreck or something else instead."

"It'll be on," her mother said.

Sure enough, the news anchorman, seated next to an anchorwoman, started off the broadcast by saying, "Two state senators face indictment on corruption charges. Another major snowstorm is on its way. And at Longwood Middle School, a seventh-grade honor student may be expelled for bringing the wrong lunch to school by mistake."

So Celeste didn't know everything.

As she waited for the first segment to be over, the one about the two state senators, Sierra had a thought she had never had before: *Every story on the news is about someone who is a real person.* Those state senators were probably sitting in their houses, smelling a casserole in the oven, maybe with their feet up on the coffee table, watching themselves on TV. Maybe their kids were watching, too, feeling awful that people were saying bad things about their dad, the same dad who had coached their soccer team and helped with math homework.

Although weather usually came late in the news, the snowstorm was predicted to be disruptive enough that the next story segment was devoted to the preparations being made all over the Denver metro area.

A commercial came on for a car dealership having a big January clearance sale. Then the news anchorwoman said: "In the hustle and bustle of busy school mornings, it's easy for family members to grab the wrong lunch by mistake. But at Longwood Middle School, a lunch bag mix-up might mean big trouble for one seventh grader."

Then there was Sierra, on the screen, standing outside the school explaining to the blond reporter what had happened.

She should have combed her hair.

Was her mouth really that wide?

She hadn't realized that her voice was so high, like she was still in elementary school.

"The principal at Longwood Middle School, Thomas A. Besser, has refused to talk to 9NEWS," the reporter's voice-over continued as the camera panned the familiar front of the building, with the students streaming out the doors to waiting buses and cars. "But we were able to obtain a copy of the school's zero-tolerance policy put in place by Principal Besser three years ago."

The text of the policy appeared on the screen, the relevant section highlighted in yellow: "All students bringing drugs or weapons of any kind onto school grounds for any reason without prior written permission will be expelled."

Sierra's face filled the screen again.

"I think it was unfair. It's completely unfair."

The camera zoomed even closer as her eyes began to fill with tears.

"Unfair? Or a reasonable strategy to keep students safe? Go to our viewer comments section on our Web site and leave your thoughts. More details on this story tonight at ten."

Another commercial came on.

"Wow," Em said.

"Did I look okay, or did I look stupid? Did my mouth look funny to you? Sort of twitching?"

"You looked great. Like—that was *you*. On TV."

"Do you think Colin watched it?"

"Who's Colin?" her mother asked.

"Nobody," Sierra said.

The phone rang. Colin? *I just wanted to say that I saw you on TV.* Mr. Besser? *I see now how wrong I've been.* Another reporter?

Sierra's mom answered it. "Yes, hon, we've been watching." So it was her dad. There was a long pause on her mother's end of the phone. Then: "You're kidding. Already?"

She turned to Sierra. "Eighty-seven people have already logged on to the station Web site. All of them think the school is being ridiculous." Another pause. "Okay, I'll tell her . . . Okay, I won't wait up. Love you."

Sierra's mother put down the phone. "Your father thinks Mr. Besser is going to have to back down now. The publicity is just too terrible. He said you should plan on going to your regular classes tomorrow."

Em hugged Sierra. "See? I told you they couldn't expel you, didn't I?"

The phone rang another time.

Sierra's mother picked it up. "Hello? . . . No, Sierra can't talk to any more reporters today. I'm sorry. She needs to do her homework."

As soon as her mother hung up, the phone rang yet again.

"I'm turning it off," her mother said. "Enough is enough. Em, do you want to stay for dinner?"

"I'd better go, I guess." To Sierra she whispered,

"Does Colin know your cell phone number? Text me if you hear from him."

Once Em had left, Sierra snatched up Cornflake and carried the cat to the couch. Cornflake's lazy, contented purr seeped into her chest. She felt more tired than she had ever been before in her life.

13

Sierra reported to the office the next morning fifteen minutes before the first bell. If Ms. Lin or Mr. Besser said she could go back to class, she wanted to arrive at first period early so that she could talk to her accelerated language arts teacher and find out what assignments she had missed.

Ms. Lin looked up, wooden-faced, as Sierra came through the door. Until two days ago, she would at least have given Sierra a tight-lipped version of her parent smile.

"You can go on back." Ms. Lin nodded in the direction of the suspension room.

Maybe Mr. Besser wasn't in yet; he might be too busy talking to reporters himself. Should Sierra ask Ms. Lin if she could wait for him here?

"Go on," Ms. Lin said. "Go." She could have been shooing a dog away from her flower beds.

Didn't Ms. Lin watch TV? Didn't she know how bad

Longwood Middle School was looking right now? By the time Sierra had gone to bed, 482 people had posted comments on the three local news Web sites; of those, only four people—four!—had thought the school had done the right thing.

At breakfast that morning her father hadn't given her any specific instructions about what to do. He had just said, "I know one middle school principal who must be feeling like a royal, class-A jerk this morning." Only he hadn't said "jerk."

Sierra didn't dare disobey Ms. Lin. She started down the hallway—surely, Mr. Besser would come find her there once he arrived at school. Then she heard the main office door open, followed by the sound of Mr. Besser's booming voice.

"Cold out there! Let's hope the snow holds off until after dismissal."

She turned around.

"Mr. Besser?"

One look at the muscles tightening in his jaw, and she could feel the hopeful smile freezing on her face.

"Sierra."

He took two steps toward her.

"You can tell your father," he said, "that he has destroyed any chance he might have had of avoiding next Friday's hearing. We might have been able to work something out"—he certainly hadn't said any such thing yesterday—"but now, with media from all around the country leaping all over this thing, our hands are tied. *Tied.* Did you hear that?"

Sierra made herself nod.

"Ask your father if he's ever heard of *behind-the-scenes* negotiations. Ask him if he's ever heard of settling things *off camera.* Will you do that for me?"

Sierra nodded again.

She wanted to say, *Did you check the Internet? 482 comments? Four for you, 478 for me?*

But she had never said a rude thing to a grownup in her life, and she didn't know how to start now. She needed Tiffany. But Tiffany's in-school suspension had ended yesterday.

Without another word, Mr. Besser went into his inner sanctum and shut the door.

"Well, don't just stand there gaping like a goldfish," Ms. Lin snapped.

Sierra fled to the suspension room before Ms. Lin could gloat over the hot tears that stung her eyes and threatened to escape down her burning cheeks.

"Hey."

Luke dropped down in the seat beside her. "Are you crying?"

"No!" Sierra jerked her hand across her eyes. She tried to change the subject. "Isn't Mitch coming today?"

"He just got a one-day suspension. Because he told them I started it."

"*Did* you start it?"

"Depends on what you mean by starting it. I hit him first. But he said something to me before that."

"What did he say?"

"Something I didn't feel like listening to. You *are* crying."

Sierra gave up pretending and pulled a tissue from her purse to blow her nose. "I'm just so mad. My father said they'd have to back down because I was on TV and all."

She wondered if Luke had seen her on the news.

"But Mr. Besser said now they can't back down. *Because* I was on TV. He said all these awful things I'm supposed to tell my father. Why doesn't he call him and say them himself?"

"You were on TV?"

So Luke hadn't watched it.

"Uh-huh. And, like, almost five hundred people wrote in on the TV Web sites, and they all said Mr. Besser is an idiot. All of them. So how come he still thinks he's right?"

"Because he's an idiot?"

Sierra couldn't laugh.

"What will I do if I really get expelled? I'll never get into college. I'll never get a job."

"Wrong."

"How would *you* feel if *you* were expelled?"

"For something stupid? I wouldn't care."

"You would. Anybody would!"

Ms. Lin stuck her head in the door. "Keep it down, you two. This is supposed to be a *suspension*. If you can't talk quietly, there'll be no talking at all. And you, Mr. Bishop, you put that thing away." She pointed to the Game Boy that Luke had placed in front of him on the table. Then she gave Sierra and Luke a final glare before disappearing down the hallway.

"Bitch," Sierra said under her breath.

It was the first time in her life she had ever said that word.

"Whoa, Shep-turd," Luke said. "Somebody is developing an attitude."

"That's right," Sierra said. "Somebody is."

14

Sierra didn't make any more note cards about Mayan temples that morning.

What was the point?

If she was really going to be expelled, driven from Longwood Middle School forever in disgrace because she had grabbed the wrong lunch off the kitchen counter, she wouldn't be handing in her Mayan culture report for social studies, or writing her *Lord of the Flies* paper for accelerated language arts, or firing her pot in the art-class kiln.

It was Friday now; the pots were going to be fired today.

Sierra thought of her pot. She had worked so hard on it, shaping each clay coil with such precision and care. Now it was sitting on the classroom counter abandoned, as the other pots, made by the nonsuspended students, were carried away to be glazed and fired so they'd last forever like the Mayan pottery she wasn't writing about anymore in her Mayan culture report.

For the second time that morning, Sierra's eyes stung with tears.

Luke looked up from whatever he was killing and dismembering in his game.

"What is it now?"

"I didn't get to fire my pot today," Sierra told him.

Luke shook his head as if to clear some obstruction from his ears that was keeping him from hearing her properly. "*You* smoke *pot*?"

"Not that kind of pot! The clay pot I was making in art class. Today was the day it was supposed to go to the kiln to be fired."

Luke still looked puzzled. "And you're crying about it?"

Sierra nodded. "I loved my pot."

"You loved your pot," Luke repeated. "Okay."

"You don't love anything about school, do you?" Not that it was any of her business, but if she wasn't going to be trying to keep up with her schoolwork anymore, what else was there to do except make herself sad over her poor, orphaned pot or talk to Luke Bishop?

"Can't say that I do."

"Did you ever? Like in kindergarten? Did you like being in the Pilgrim play at Thanksgiving? Or making a cast of your hand in plaster of paris to give your parents at Christmas?"

"I liked one day," Luke said. "It was called Backwards Day. We put our clothes on backwards, and zipped up our coats in the back and not the front. The parent helpers zipped them up for us, because we couldn't reach in the back. And the whole day went in backwards order. We started with resting time instead of ending with resting time, and we ended with the Pledge of Allegiance instead of starting with it. I thought it was totally cool, Backwards Day."

"So what happened after that? To make you stop liking school?"

Luke shrugged. "The rest was all Forwards Days. I don't do so well on Forwards Days."

"But you're smart," Sierra said.

"How would you know?"

"I can tell. The way you talk. You talk like you're smart. So you could do well in school if you tried."

"Maybe I don't want to try. Or maybe I can't try. My parents had me tested back in second grade. For ADD. Because I could never settle down and listen to the teacher droning on about subtraction or the names for all the different kinds of clouds."

"Nimbus. Cirrus. Cumulus," Sierra recited. "Don't you like to know the names of things? Do you just want to go around saying 'cloud'? Or 'big white puffy cloud'?"

"It was the way the teachers did it. Like the only reason to learn about clouds was to tell it back to them on a quiz so you could get a grade on your report card, and maybe if you got enough good grades on your report card, your parents would take you to McDonald's and buy you a Happy Meal."

"So did you have ADD? When they tested you?"

"They said I did. But maybe the teachers just had VBD."

Sierra tried to decode what the initials could mean.

"Very boring disorder."

Sierra laughed.

"Did they give you medication?" she asked.

"My parents got in a big fight about it. My father was like, 'You're not going to put my kid on drugs just for being a hundred percent all-American boy.' And my mother was like, 'We have to do something, I can't take this anymore.'"

"So who won?"

"Nobody. The medication didn't help anyway, and then my parents split up. You know how parents tell their kids, when they're getting divorced, 'Now, remember, honey, this isn't because of you, it's about Mommy and Daddy'? Well, guess what. It was because of me. Because they couldn't stand fighting about me. Are your parents divorced?"

"No. My friend Lexi's parents are, though. She lives during the week with her mom, and on the weekends with her dad."

"I live with my dad. Because my mom really couldn't take it. She wasn't kidding. She married someone else, and they moved to California and have two kids now. I see her for a couple of weeks in the summer, and then she sends me back. It's okay."

"Does your dad care that you're suspended?"

"Not really. He would have fought someone, too, for calling him a name."

"What did Mitch call you?"

"What are you, a lawyer like your dad?"

It was the second time she had asked Luke that question and he hadn't answered.

"Besides," Sierra went on, "*you* call people names. You call me names."

"Shep-turd isn't really a name."

"No?"

"It's like—a play on words. It's supposed to be funny."

"Ha ha," Sierra said.

"Okay, I won't call you that anymore. Didn't you ever call someone a name? Even just behind their back?"

Sierra thought for a minute. "No." It was hard to believe, but she had never called anyone a name, ever.

"Except when you called Lintbag a bitch."

"Oh," Sierra said. She gave Luke a small smile. "I guess there was that."

15

Sierra hadn't brought her lunch—she had really thought she'd be back eating in the cafeteria with her friends, constantly interrupted by all the kids who wanted to tell her how they had seen her on TV. So when Ms. Lin came into the suspension room at the start of 4A, Sierra got up from the table and walked with Luke to the door.

"They're all yours," Ms. Lin told Mrs. Saunders.

Mrs. Saunders gave Sierra a reassuring smile as she got up from her desk, which was next to Ms. Lin's. It was obvious that Ms. Lin was the head secretary and Mrs. Saunders was her underling. What a fun job that would be, under Ms. Lin's thumb all day, doing whatever she told you to do and smiling while you did it.

Mrs. Saunders looked older than Ms. Lin, her hair gray and spiky in a way that made her look as if she could be funny and fun.

"I'm sorry about what happened," Mrs. Saunders

said to Sierra while the three of them were heading down the hall.

The kindness in her voice caught Sierra off guard, but Sierra was not going to let her eyes start filling with tears in the hallway of Longwood Middle School.

"Thanks," Sierra managed to say.

"I hope something can be worked out," Mrs. Saunders said.

"Me too." Not that Sierra could see any way that could be possible.

As they entered the cafeteria, Sierra passed Sandy sitting on her stool, yelling "Keep it down!" to some kids who were getting too rowdy. How different everything would have been if Sandy had told her to put the knife back in the lunch bag and call her parents to come right away and get it.

Colin's lunch period was 4A. Sierra saw him before he saw her. He was sitting at a table by the window—actually, the same table where Sierra and her friends ate lunch every day during 5B. She made a mental note of the chair where he was sitting, the chair closest to the window.

As if drawn by her gaze, he looked in her direction.

Then he was getting up from his seat and walking toward her.

"Hey, Sierra," he said as she reached the front of the lunch line.

Ms. Lin wouldn't have let her talk to anyone; Sierra

was sure of that. But Mrs. Saunders didn't do anything to stop Colin from continuing.

"I made a petition."

Sierra saw that Colin held in his hand several sheets of lined paper. The top one was completely covered with names.

Colin read to her: "We, the undersigned, believe that it is unfair to punish a student who brought a knife to school by mistake and turned it in as soon as she found it."

"I'll have the tuna melt sandwich," Sierra told the lady behind the lunch counter.

To Colin she said, "That's awesome."

Colin flipped through the three pages. "Eighty-seven people have signed it so far."

He held the petition out to Sierra. "You can sign it, too, you know."

Was it strange to sign a petition that was all about you? Like voting for yourself in an election? But then again, the news always showed presidential candidates on election morning going to the polls to vote for themselves.

Colin produced a pen. Sierra signed. Number eighty-eight.

"Luke, you want to sign?" Colin asked.

Luke hesitated for a second. "Sure. But it won't do any good."

He scrawled his name almost illegibly: number eighty-nine.

"What about you, Mrs. Saunders?" Colin asked politely.

"I wish I could, but I don't think it would be the best idea."

"Are you going to ask Lintbag and Buttster to sign it?" Luke jeered.

"No," Colin said as if Luke had asked a serious question. "But four teachers have already signed. And it's just fourth period. I want to collect as many signatures as I can today, so I can give the petition to Mr. Besser after school and he'll have it to look at this weekend."

"We'd better get back," Mrs. Saunders said, not unkindly. "And, Colin? In case those television reporters are here again today after school, the way they were yesterday, they might like to see your petition, too."

"Thanks! You're the best!" Colin said. "I'm practically done with lunch, so I'm going to take this around to all the tables now. I have a friend who eats 4B, and he'll take it from there, and maybe we can find someone for 5A. Sierra, Lex is doing 5B."

As Sierra and Luke followed Mrs. Saunders back to the suspension room carrying their cafeteria trays, Sierra asked Mrs. Saunders, "Do you think the petition really might help?"

"I don't know. It can't hurt."

Outside the large windows flanking the office, the first flakes of snow were beginning to fall.

"This is supposed to be a big storm," Mrs. Saunders said. "I hope everyone gets home safely."

Back in the suspension room, Sierra took a first bite of her sandwich. Tuna melt was one of the best things on the school lunch menu, but she was almost too excited to eat, thinking about Colin.

"Is he your boyfriend?" Luke asked as if reading her thoughts.

"No."

"Then what's it to him if you're suspended or expelled?"

"Because it's *unfair.* It's *wrong.*"

"He likes you."

Oh, Sierra hoped Luke was right.

"But it's not going to do any good," Luke said. "It's not like Besser will look at a bunch of kids' names on a piece of paper and say, 'Gee, I guess I *was* a dumbhead.'"

Oh, Sierra hoped Luke was wrong.

16

It was already snowing hard by the dismissal bell at 3:10. The lawn stretching in front of Longwood Middle School was white, but the long driveway curving up in front of the school was still bare.

Sierra saw her mother's Volvo station wagon parked again in the NO STOPPING OR STANDING zone. *Go, Mom.* Parked nearby were the same three TV news vans. And standing under an umbrella held over him by the same blond reporter from yesterday was Colin, showing her a sheaf of papers that must be the petition.

Slowly Sierra walked over to them, glad that she had combed her hair in the girls' room before heading outside, and glad that her blue angora-wool hat, angle adjusted in the girls' room mirror, matched the color of her eyes.

"Sierra!" the blond reporter greeted her. "What do you think of the petition signed by three hundred and seventy-nine of your fellow students?"

She held the microphone toward Sierra.

Wow. That was over half the school, in just one day.

"I think it's great," Sierra said. She wanted to say something to thank Colin, but not make it too gushy. "Colin's a really good friend to do this for me."

Did "friend" sound too much like "just a friend," as in "not a boyfriend"? And she didn't want to imply that Colin had done this for *her,* as if she thought he liked her more than he did.

"I mean, I think it's wonderful that he stood up for me." No, that sounded wrong, too. "I mean, that he saw that there was injustice and he did something about it. He didn't just go, 'Oh, well.' He did something."

She was babbling. She had to stop talking about Colin and how wonderful he was.

"Colin, this is a photocopy," the blond reporter said. "You gave the original petition to Mr. Besser, is that correct? To the school principal?"

"I couldn't give it to him in person because he was in a meeting, so I left it with the school secretary, Ms. Lin."

The reporter looked disappointed; she must have been hoping to hear Mr. Besser's reaction. Sierra was disappointed, too. What if Ms. Lin never even gave the petition to Mr. Besser? What if she ripped it up and threw it away?

"Are those three hundred and seventy-nine signatures all from students?" the reporter asked.

"No, eight teachers signed it, too."

"So teachers are joining the protest now," the reporter said. "Sierra, do you think the petition is going to help?"

Did she think it would help? If hundreds of comments by grownups on the station Web sites hadn't helped, would hundreds of signatures from kids make any difference? But poor Colin had tried so hard; his efforts had to count for something.

"I do," Sierra said. "I mean, I hope so."

She shouldn't keep saying "I mean."

"I mean, it should help."

There, she had just done it again. But maybe it didn't matter. Colin looked away from the blond reporter and the cameraman and smiled at her.

She and Colin Beauvoir were going to be on the nightly news together.

Sierra's father was home in time to watch the news broadcasts with Sierra and her mother. The Wilson case had settled at the last minute late the night before and didn't end up going to trial after all. Sierra knew from experience that this was usually the way it happened with her father's cases. On the eve of the court date, everyone suddenly began cooperating. Her father was very good at persuading people to do whatever they needed to do to avoid having to face him in the courtroom.

Sierra had thought her father would be furious when he learned she had been kept in suspension for another day, but he wasn't.

"I can play hardball, too," was all he said. "You might say that hardball is my specialty."

She had to tell him what Mr. Besser had said that morning. "Daddy? Mr. Besser said that all the media coverage is just making things worse, that he could have worked something out with us, but now he can't, because his hands are tied. That's what he said, that now his hands are tied."

To Sierra's surprise, her father gave a scornful laugh. "And if he expects us to believe that, he's a whole lot dumber than I thought he was. The only reason anything is going to be worked out here is if we make it impossible for him not to play the game our way."

Sierra's mother served dinner in front of the TV in the family room—homemade pizza with all kinds of cut-up roasted veggies on top.

Once again, the Longwood Middle School knife story was announced as one of the headline stories on 9NEWS: "Two days after an honor student's lunch-bag mistake has her facing expulsion, the student body mobilizes in protest while school officials scramble to defend their policy."

"'Scramble.' That's good," Sierra's dad said, putting his arm around her as she sat in a cozy sandwich between her two parents, with Cornflake purring against her feet. "Yes, I'd say it's scrambling time for Tom Besser right now."

The snowstorm was the top story of the day: four car accidents already, with rush hour still under way.

"I've been thinking," Sierra's mother said, setting her half-eaten slice of pizza back on her plate as the TV screen showed a helicopter-view of traffic at a standstill amid whirling snow on I-25. "Beautiful Mountain School? That alternative private school that focuses on the arts? I called them today, and they have openings."

Sierra's father hit the mute button on the remote.

"You can't be serious," he said.

"There's no harm in looking at it. I thought I'd just go over there on Monday to see what it's like."

Sierra turned imploringly to her father. She couldn't change schools. She couldn't leave Lexi and Em—and Colin.

"Angie," her father said to her mother, obviously struggling to keep his voice even. "Longwood Middle School has the highest test scores in the district. Those alternative schools are artsy-fartsy nonsense. Strictly for fruits and nuts."

"Sierra is very artistic. She loves to paint and to sing and to write."

"And to *think*."

"I'm sure they think at Beautiful Mountain," Sierra's mother shot back. "They think enough that they wouldn't expel a student for an innocent mistake." She corrected herself: "For her mother's innocent mistake."

"Sierra is going to be reinstated. She is going to receive a public apology. Give me a few more days, and you're going to turn on the TV and hear, 'Middle school

92

principal backs down in lunch-bag-knife incident.' Believe me."

"Maybe Sierra would like to try something different. Do you want her to continue going to a school that would suspend her, for two days already, over nothing?"

"That's me, it's on now," Sierra said, grateful to have a reason to interrupt her parents. She hated when her father used that tone with her mother. But she didn't want to switch schools; she didn't want to try something different. She wanted her life back the way it used to be.

Her father clicked the sound on.

This time Mr. Besser himself appeared on the screen. He must have decided that it was better to make his case directly to the media rather than let them say whatever they wanted about him, without any reply on his part.

Sitting behind his desk in the inner sanctum, he repeated the same justifications for zero tolerance that he had given to Sierra and her parents, in almost the exact same words. His bald head glistened beneath the bright television lights.

"Am I sorry this happened? You bet I am. Would I be even sorrier if we had laxer policies and instead of covering this tiny incident you were filming the aftermath of a school massacre? Yes, I would."

"Give me a break," Sierra's father said. "He doesn't even believe that crap himself."

Sierra's face filled the screen next. Her blue hat did look good, she had to admit.

Then Colin appeared, talking about the petition.

"So that's Colin," Sierra's mother said.

Sierra felt her face flushing. *Yes, that was Colin.*

"Do you think the petition will help?" Sierra asked her dad after the segment ended.

He gave a snort. "Not a chance."

So her father thought more like Luke Bishop than like Colin Beauvoir.

"So what's going to happen?" Sierra asked. "How is it all going to turn out okay?"

"Leave it to me, honey," her father said. "And, Angie, why don't you just forget about the fruits and nuts at Pretty Mountain?"

He clicked off the TV. "Leave it all to me."

17

Sierra drifted awake toward nine o'clock on Saturday morning, suddenly aware of the utter silence of the world outside her bedroom window. She knew it was still snowing simply from the softness of the silence, broken only by the sound of Cornflake's barely audible purr beside her in her tangle of bedcovers.

Her mother appeared with breakfast on a tray, as if Sierra were sick rather than facing expulsion from school.

"Here."

Sierra sat herself up against her pillows as her mother set the bed tray over her blanketed legs.

"How about some cream-cheese-stuffed waffles with fresh strawberries? And hot chocolate?"

"I love you, Mom."

"I love you too, honey bun."

Her mother perched on the edge of the bed as Sierra ate. The waffles were light and golden, the cream-cheese filling sweet and slightly tart at the same time, the strawberries remarkably red and ripe for January.

Sierra took a long sip of hot chocolate and wiped her mouth with the yellow-flowered cloth napkin.

"Honey?" her mother said then. "Do you want to stay at Longwood Middle School? If they let you stay?"

"Uh-huh. I have my friends, and Leadership Club, and choir."

And this boy I like.

"You'd meet friends anywhere. You're good at making friends."

"Friends aren't like that. You don't switch them like a pair of shoes."

"I know, sweetheart, but still, I wouldn't choose a school just because of friends."

Why not? "Besides, Daddy says Longwood is the best academically." Sierra swallowed another bite of waffle. "Do *you* want me to switch schools?"

Her mother picked up the cat brush on the nightstand next to Sierra's bed and began brushing Cornflake, who stretched himself out luxuriously to make the most of every stroke.

"Your father's a fighter. I'm not. There's a lot to be said for being somewhere where you don't have to fight. From what I read on their Web site, the educational philosophy at Beautiful Mountain is based on peaceful principles—cooperation, not competition. And I like that it focuses on creativity and the arts."

Her mother's confidential tone made Sierra feel that she could ask the question: "Why did you marry Daddy? You two are so different."

"Well, that's what they say, that opposites attract. The short answer is that I married your father because I loved him. I still love him."

"But what made you start loving him in the first place?"

Sierra's mother continued to brush the cat, who had now rolled over onto his other side.

"When we met, he was already in law school, and I was an undergrad. Even then I was trying to write plays, and he came to a student showcase where my first one-act play was having a reading."

"But Daddy doesn't even like plays."

"He came with a friend, James, who did like plays, or at least liked girls who wrote plays, or at least liked me."

"And . . . ?"

"I heard someone in the audience laugh at the wrong place—well, it was the right place, it was a funny part, but he laughed a couple of seconds too late, like he didn't get it until the moment had already passed. And then when I met him afterward, I was intrigued, because he was so confident—handsome, too, and charming, but mainly so confident. But he had laughed at the wrong time. It was sort of touching. Like he had this one little vulnerability. Like I was going to be the chink in his armor, or maybe I was going to be the one to get through the chink in his armor. Anyway, even though I was dating James, your father asked me out, and I went, and then I married him."

Sierra lay back against her propped-up pillows, the last bit of waffle settling into her contented stomach.

"Do you still think of him that way? Like he has chinks in his armor?"

Sierra couldn't see any chinks at all.

"Everyone has chinks in their armor."

"Even Daddy? What chinks in his armor does he have now?"

Her mother stood up. "He has you. Believe me, he has no defenses where you're concerned."

She lifted the tray from the bed. "The chink in his armor is loving you."

18

Sierra worked on her Mayan culture report after break-fast and had the first draft finished by noon. If she wasn't going to be expelled—and she really would like to know which it was going to be—she wanted to catch up on all her work and still earn A's in everything for the quarter. She wished she hadn't gotten that one B last year in earth science, even though the reporter made it sound like it was an amazing thing to have only one B for your whole time in middle school.

After lunch—lentil soup that had smelled delicious simmering on the stove all morning—Sierra's parents headed off for an afternoon movie date; Sierra's dad had called ahead to make sure the theater was still open de-spite the weather. It would take more than a snowstorm to keep her father at home if he had an outing planned. He always did fun things with Sierra and her mother after a big case settled, overcome with jubilation at winning.

Sierra knew that most of the time, for her father, "settlement" was another word for "victory."

Before reading through her Mayan report on her laptop to see if it still looked as worthy of an A+ as it had half an hour ago, Sierra checked her e-mail.

She had a message from Mr. Lydgate, the teacher who directed all the Longwood choirs, including the Octave. It was flagged with a red exclamation mark and with the subject heading GOOD NEWS all in caps.

And she had one from Colin, who had never e-mailed her before: cbeauvoir.

She liked that he didn't have some lame-attempt-at-being-cool e-mail address like colinthegreat or colinrocks.

For a moment she wondered what Luke Bishop's e-mail address would be.

She opened Colin's message first. It was written all in lowercase:

> hi, sierra.
> did you see us on tv? do i look that geeky in real life? choir news is great. hope you can go.
> colin

Sierra almost felt like forwarding it to Em so that they could analyze it together.

The absence of capitals: Did that mean that Colin

was too lazy to use the shift key? Or was it sort of the e-mail equivalent of his talking in that soft voice?

did you see us on tv? The "us" in that sentence made Sierra's heart flap inside her chest like a caged humming-bird.

do i look that geeky in real life? Sierra hadn't realized that a boy could think that way. No, Colin did not look geeky in real life, or on TV, or only in an adorable way.

choir news is great. What choir news? Oh, that other e-mail.

hope you can go. Did this have to do with the choir news? Did "hope you can go" mean that Colin wanted her to be there, wherever "there" was?

colin. Not *love, colin.* But of course he wouldn't put *love, colin.* There was really no other way he could have signed it except for *colin.* Maybe he could have used his initials: *cb. colin* was better.

There, she had done a pretty good job of analyzing it all on her own. She'd tell Em about the e-mail, of course she would, but she was glad now she hadn't forwarded it to her. It was too personal, too precious, to share.

She hated to close the screen, but she had to see what the great choir news was that Colin had written about.

Mr. Lydgate had written to the eight members of the Octave, including Sierra, Celeste, and Colin. The choir had been selected before Christmas as an alternate to perform at the big music educators' conference this coming Friday in Colorado Springs. Now Mr. Lydgate was writing to say that the winning choir had to cancel at the last minute, so the Octave would be performing in their place. Mr. Lydgate wanted them all to e-mail him ASAP to let him know if they could come.

Yes! Of course she could go, even if it meant missing school all day on Friday.

No.

She couldn't go.

Friday was the day of her hearing.

That's what Colin had meant by "hope you can go."

Mr. Besser had to let her go, he just had to.

She e-mailed Colin back. She used proper capitalization in her e-mail; she didn't want him to think she was copying his style.

Hi, Colin.
You didn't look geeky on TV. You looked great.
Choir news is terrific. I hope I can go, too.
Sierra

She sent it before she could change her mind.

Should she have said he looked great? She could have left it at "You didn't look geeky."

She called up her message to Colin from her Sent folder and read it over again. It was probably okay.

As she was about to close her e-mail, another message came in from Mr. Lydgate. This time it was just to Sierra.

Mr. Lydgate said he was going to talk to Mr. Besser and "see what could be done."

Sierra wrote back a two-word answer: "Thank you."

And then she started praying.

Dear God, please make Mr. Besser let me go to the concert. Dear God, please please please make it be that I can go.

19

Celeste called while Sierra's parents were still at their movie.

"Did you get Mr. Lydgate's e-mail about the choir trip?" Celeste asked.

"Uh-huh."

"What if they don't let you go?"

What was Sierra supposed to say? Was this a setup for more condescending pity? "Then I guess I won't go."

"It's not that simple, Sierra! What if we can't go if somebody is missing? If there're just seven of us, not eight? What kind of Octave is that?"

Sudden fury surged from Sierra's throbbing chest into her burning face.

"So that's all you care about? If *you* get to go? *I'm* getting *expelled* for something that wasn't even my fault, my whole life is being *destroyed*, and what you care about is how it affects *you*? If it inconveniences *you*?"

"It's not an *inconvenience* if the choir can't go," Celeste said in her most infuriating calm, patient tone, as if she were explaining something to a misbehaving toddler. "We've been practicing for months and months—two mornings every single week at seven a.m. And then we got so close to being picked, but had to be the stupid alternate, and now we finally, finally, get this chance . . . I mean, Sierra, it does affect everyone if you can't go and then the whole thing gets canceled."

Sierra was afraid she might say something so terrible to Celeste that she could never unsay it, never be able to take it back and pretend she hadn't really meant it after all.

"Well, I'm sorry if my getting expelled is such a huge drag for you," she said carefully.

"Come on, Sierra, don't be that way." Celeste made it sound as if Sierra was the one being selfish and unreasonable. "If it was reversed, if I was the one who got suspended, and you were the one who might not get to go on the biggest and most important choir trip ever, you can't tell me you wouldn't be disappointed."

"I wouldn't *blame* you."

"Who said anything about blaming anybody? Except—Sierra, you could have checked before you took the wrong lunch. It would have taken like two seconds to check, and then none of this would have happened."

"So you check your lunch every single day to make sure it's the right one?"

"No, but I don't have the same lunch bag as my

mom, either. Look, I didn't mean to get you all upset," Celeste said.

"I'm not upset."

"Yes, you are."

"Well, if you were getting expelled, maybe you'd be a tiny bit upset, too."

Sierra knew Celeste was thinking: *But I would never be getting expelled.*

Only a few days ago, Sierra would have thought the same thing.

"Well, maybe you won't get expelled, and it will all work out okay," Celeste said, her voice bright and chipper, as if they were back to being friends again. "And maybe on Friday we'll be in Colorado Springs, all of us singing together."

"Maybe," Sierra said.

Maybe.

It was almost dinnertime before Sierra's parents got home from their movie date.

"I don't know how there can be people who live in Colorado and don't know how to drive in snow," Sierra's father grumbled as he came into the family room where Sierra was watching some old movie on TV.

"Are the roads really bad?" Sierra asked, clicking off the TV.

"The roads are bad; the other drivers are worse."

"Was the movie good?"

"Your mother liked it."

"You liked it, too," her mother said.

"I didn't like *it*. I liked seeing it with *you*." He smiled at Sierra's mother.

Maybe they were still in love, different as they were, even after all these years.

"Daddy?"

"What happened now?"

Sierra told him about the choir trip. "Daddy, I really, really, really want to go. I have to go. And Celeste says if one person can't go, the whole trip might have to be canceled. I mean, the name of our choir is the Octave. You really have to have eight people to be an octave."

"Maybe that wouldn't be such a bad thing, if the trip got canceled. Let Tom Besser see what his policies have wrought, what opportunities his students are losing out on because of his sanctimonious, self-righteous, irrational, zero-sense, zero-decency crapola."

"But that wouldn't be fair to the others," Sierra said. "Mr. Besser shouldn't punish the whole entire Octave, and Mr. Lydgate, too, because of one student's mistake."

"There're a lot of things Tom Besser shouldn't be doing right now," her father said.

"I'm going to take some chili out of the freezer, okay?" Sierra's mother said. "And throw together some cornbread muffins to go with it. I think that would be a good supper for a snowy night, don't you?"

"Sure, hon." Then to Sierra he said, "Just give me a few more days, sweetheart. One way or another, your Mr. Besser is going to be one sorry, sorry dude."

20

On Sunday Sierra turned down an invitation from Em and Lexi to go sledding on the steep hill behind the high school. She wanted to stay at home to listen for the phone, sure that Mr. Lydgate was going to call to say that he had convinced Mr. Besser to let her go to the choir concert. Or maybe Mr. Besser himself would call to lift her suspension altogether. How could he not listen to almost four hundred students and eight teachers? As well as practically half the state of Colorado?

But every phone call was another reporter calling for another quote to enliven the continuing coverage of the story. Sierra didn't want to talk to them anymore, but her father said it was good "to keep Tom Besser's feet to the fire."

"Yes, I'm still doing all my homework so I can catch up if they let me go back to class," she told the reporter for the *Denver Post*.

"There's a big choir trip I really don't want to miss," she told the Associated Press.

A reporter from a newspaper she had never heard of asked her if she thought students should be allowed to bring weapons to school.

"No, but no one should be expelled just for making an honest mistake."

She felt bored hearing herself say the same things over and over again, in the same words, in the same earnest, sincere tone of voice. This was something she had never guessed: that being famous would be so boring.

School was open on Monday. It took more than a foot and a half of new-fallen snow to close schools in Colorado, especially when the snow plows had all day Sunday to ready the roads for rush-hour traffic.

Two new kids arrived in the suspension room shortly after the first bell—both eighth-grade boys. Sierra learned that the short one with the sharp, ferret-featured face had swiped a handful of candy bars on Friday when the jazz band's snack-sale table had been left unattended; the tall, dark-complexioned one had spray-painted an obscenity on the outside wall of the gym late Sunday night and been seen by a neighbor who called the police.

My new friends, thought Sierra.

"What did you do?" Shoplifter Brad asked Luke and Sierra.

"I got in a fight," Luke said.

"I brought a knife to school," Sierra said.

She didn't add any explanations. There was a bizarre delight in representing herself as so openly, brazenly bad.

Brad looked at her with new respect, but Graffiti Artist Julio said, "She's the one who was on TV."

Brad didn't look any less impressed. Televised coverage didn't make a crime any less sensational.

"Wow," he said.

"Yeah, it's pretty cool to be suspended with a big celebrity," Luke sneered. "The perfect honor student who never did anything wrong in her life, and look how *unfair* it is that someone like *her* should get in trouble."

Last Friday, when it had been just the two of them, Sierra had felt that she was starting to get to know Luke a little bit and even like him a little bit. Why was he being so hateful now?

"What got into you?" she asked.

"Nothing. Look, if you want to give Brad and Julio your autograph, go right ahead. I don't need one, though, so you can spare the muscles in your hand."

Sitting where Luke couldn't see him, Julio gave Sierra a friendly shrug: *What's up with him?*

Luke flipped on his Game Boy and made a great pretense of not even noticing that the rest of them were there.

"Why did you steal the candy bars?" Sierra asked Brad. "Didn't you figure you'd get caught?"

"I didn't get caught the other times," Brad said.

111

She decided to ask Julio a question, too, to keep the conversation going in the face of Luke's silence. "Are you going to have to wash off your graffiti?"

"It doesn't wash off. But, yeah, I'm going to have to paint the whole side of the gym. And pay for the paint. It sucks big-time."

"Was it worth it? I mean, was it fun doing it?"

She tried to imagine what it would feel like—to be out alone at night, slipping between the pools of light beneath the lampposts, a can of spray paint hidden under her jacket, and then to write something with it for any-body driving by Longwood Middle School to see.

Luke looked up from his game. "What's it to you?" he asked Sierra.

"It's called making *polite conversation*."

"Ooh, ooh, tell me more about the bad things you did!" Luke squealed in a falsetto voice.

It was almost as if Luke was jealous, not of her, but of Brad and Julio.

"Your three-day fighting suspension ends today," she said to Luke. "Can't you be nice to me for a few more hours?"

"Yeah," Julio said, taking her side.

"Shut the frick up," Luke told him.

"You shut the frick up," Julio fired back.

She didn't have a chance to see what Luke was going to say or do next. Apparently having heard the commotion in the suspension room, Ms. Lin was there so suddenly that Luke didn't have time to whisk his Game Boy out of sight.

"*Mr.* Bishop." She made the title sound like an insult. "You can be heard all the way in the front office where Mr. Besser is having a very important meeting."

Sierra couldn't help wondering: *A very important meeting about me?*

"And *Mr.* Bishop. I believe I told you that the use of electronic devices in this room is strictly forbidden. I am going to confiscate that toy of yours and keep it locked up in my desk until school gets out in May."

Luke said nothing.

"Give that to me."

Would Luke refuse? What would Ms. Lin do if he did?

Luke hesitated. Then he threw his Game Boy down the conference table toward Ms. Lin.

"That's not fair!" Sierra burst out. "You can't keep it for months and months like that."

Ms. Lin's eyes, as they fell on Sierra, were black slits of fury.

"Ms. Shepard, I don't need you of all people to tell me what I should and should not be doing. And don't think for a minute that a petition signed by your little friends is going to make any difference whatsoever to me or Mr. Besser."

Ms. Lin snatched up Luke's Game Boy like a bird

of prey pouncing on a helpless small animal. As if to punctuate her departure, the tattered poster with the words RULES RESPECT RESPONSIBILITY RELIABILITY came loose from its tape and fluttered onto the scuffed linoleum floor.

21

Whoa, Shep-turd." Luke gave a low whistle. "I mean, Sierra. You really told her."

He was grinning at her now, his friendly Friday self again, but his eyes were glistening with some darker emotion.

Julio punched her on the shoulder in playful tribute. Brad clapped his hands three times slowly in applause.

"Well, it *is* unfair," Sierra said. "She told Luke not to let her catch him again with it, but she never said she'd take it away practically forever if he did."

"Don't worry," Luke said. "I'll get it back."

"How?" Sierra asked. "You can't just go into her desk and *take* it."

"Oh, can't I?"

Julio joined in. "Forget it. She's always at her desk. Or Saunders is there. Plus Besser walks by a hundred times a day."

"Lintbag has to go to the *bathroom*," Luke pointed

out. "She can't go all day without peeing. Besides, I don't think Saunders is here today."

"She isn't," Sierra said. She could hardly believe that she was supplying information to assist Luke in his raid. But Ms. Lin had gone too far this time. Actually, as far as Sierra was concerned, she had gone too far a long time ago.

Sierra went on, "I heard Ms. Lin say something to Mr. Besser this morning when I was coming in, that Mrs. Saunders was taking her son to get his wisdom teeth out."

Brad hadn't yet made any comment, but Sierra knew he wouldn't tell on Luke, no matter what Luke was planning to do. She would never tell on any of them, either, whatever they did in suspension.

"We'll be real quiet so we can hear if she gets up and goes anywhere," Luke said. "And then if she does, I'll slip out and grab it from her desk, just like that."

"What if she comes back while you're out there?" Sierra asked.

"You can watch out for me," Luke said.

Was he challenging her? To see whose side she was on? She already knew whose side she was on.

"Okay," Sierra said. "I will."

Even with the door to the suspension room kept open, it was hard to know exactly what was going on in the main office. Sometimes Sierra could hear Ms. Lin's voice on

116

the phone, but not loud enough to make out more than a phrase or two.

"I got it at Costco . . ."

"My sister-in-law told me last week . . ."

Ms. Lin's lack of concern about having her personal phone calls overheard suggested that Mr. Besser's meeting must be over and he was no longer in his office.

Finally, Sierra heard Ms. Lin's heels click across the floor, not coming toward the suspension room but heading in the other direction.

Sierra peeked out, Luke standing next to her. Ms. Lin was putting a sign on the glass window facing out into the front hallway. Maybe it said: BACK IN FIVE MINUTES. Then Ms. Lin left the office through the door into the front hall.

"Let's go," Luke said.

Sierra followed as Luke hurried over to Ms. Lin's desk. Her heart leaped around in her chest like a Ping-Pong ball in a clothes dryer.

Mr. Besser's office door was ajar; Sierra glanced inside and saw to her relief that he wasn't there.

She watched as Luke tried Ms. Lin's top drawer. It opened to disclose a neat tray filled with pens, paper clips, rubber bands. No Game Boy.

The side drawers were unlocked, too. In the top right-hand drawer was a stack of Longwood Middle School letterhead and envelopes. In the middle drawer was a pair of shoes, an umbrella, and a bag of wrapped butterscotch candies. Sierra felt guilty peering into Ms. Lin's private things. But not so guilty that she would abandon Luke now.

In the bottom drawer there it was: a heap of cell phones and Game Boys, as if Ms. Lin were the overlord of a crime ring that specialized in robbing electronics stores.

Luke's was right on top. He shoved it in his pocket. "Should we take the rest?"

Sierra shook her head. "What would we do with them? We don't know who they belong to. I don't think *she* even knows who they belong to."

Nothing was marked with a name or labeled in any way, though surely there were parents who came into school demanding to get back the expensive phones they were paying for. Maybe these confiscated phones belonged to kids who had lied to their parents and said that they lost them, when all the while they were in Ms. Lin's desk.

Hatred of Ms. Lin beat an erratic jungle tom-tom in Sierra's chest.

Luke idly touched a key on Ms. Lin's computer, and the screen-saver image—a safari scene—disappeared. Ms. Lin's school e-mail account was open.

Suddenly Sierra had an idea so daring she could hardly believe what she was contemplating. It would serve Ms. Lin right to find out what it was like to get in trouble when you were innocent.

"Go stand by the window and watch the hallway," Sierra told Luke, whispering even though there was no one else there to hear them.

"Let's go," Luke urged. "She's going to be back any second."

"I'm going to send an e-mail from her account."

Luke gave one harsh, hard laugh.

As Luke stood guard, Sierra began typing.

Luckily, she had been the fastest keyboarder in the computer skills class in sixth grade.

Luckily, she remembered the e-mail address by heart for the letters column for the *Denver Post*; she had sent the paper half a dozen letters in the past year.

Luckiest of all, she no longer cared very much about Longwood Middle School's supposed core values of rules, respect, responsibility, or reliability. In fact, right this minute she no longer cared about them at all.

22

"She's coming!"

Sierra had just finished deleting the new e-mail from Ms. Lin's Sent folder, so Ms. Lin would have no way of finding it on her computer.

She and Luke reached the suspension room as Ms. Lin was unlocking the office door. Sierra dropped down into the chair next to Julio's and took a few long, deep breaths to force herself to calm down.

Now that it was all over, she felt overwhelmed with her own daring, and even more with the coolness with which she had executed her revenge. She could have been a master criminal.

She *was* a master criminal!

She, Sierra Grace Shepard, had just done the most illegal and subversive act of her life, an act that even Luke Bishop hadn't thought to do.

She was crazy to have done it.

She was wrong to have done it.

But it was already done.

"Did you get your Game Boy?" Julio asked.

For answer, Luke flashed the device before hiding it back in his pocket.

Then he looked over at Sierra. She knew he wanted to ask her what e-mail she had sent from Ms. Lin's account but didn't want to talk about it in front of the others. She'd tell him when they were alone, if they were ever alone. Maybe she'd call or text him that evening.

It would feel very strange to be calling or texting Luke Bishop.

Sierra opened her library book, *The Diary of Anne Frank*. Anne Frank had also known something about being confined in a very small space with people who got on your nerves after a while. Sierra stared down at the page, but it was hard to quiet her racing heart and her scolding conscience.

So she was relieved when Luke broke the silence. "Here's a question for everybody. In your whole life, which teacher did you hate the most, and why?"

Sierra didn't hate any teachers. The only adult she had ever hated was Ms. Lin, and she had only hated her since last Wednesday. She couldn't even make herself hate Mr. Besser, remembering the tears she had seen in his eyes after the horrible meeting with her parents.

Julio took his turn first.

"Mrs. Fletcher in second grade. She could never pronounce my name right. She kept calling me Jule-ee-o, like Julius, or Julia. Like, how hard is it to say Hoo-lee-o?"

"Did you correct her?" Sierra asked.

"I tried, but she was really mean about it, like she knew better how to pronounce things than some little second grader, because *she* was the teacher, not me."

"Mrs. Nolan," Brad said, going next.

Sierra knew who Mrs. Nolan was: one of the math teachers who taught the lowest-level math classes, not the accelerated math sequence that Sierra was taking.

"She made me go to the board for some dumb-ass problem. A whole bunch of us were up there, writing problems on the board. I got the answer wrong. Two girls did, too, and she didn't make fun of them, but to me she said, 'Do you want to repeat sixth-grade math, Bradley? I didn't realize you liked my math class so much that you'd want to stay with me next year.'"

"What did you say?" Sierra asked, appalled.

"I said her class sucked, and math sucked, and she sucked."

"Then what happened?"

"That was my first suspension. She did fail me for that quarter, but I passed for the year, so I never had to be in class with her again."

Sierra still didn't know what she was going to say when it was her turn, so she was glad when Luke spoke.

"I hated them all except for Miss Boyle in kindergarten; she was cool. But the worst was Mrs. Bieber in third grade. She wanted to help the rest of the class understand why I was so *difficult*, so they'd have *compassion* for me instead of being pissed off at me all the time.

"So she told them all, 'Luke has a condition called ADD.' She wrote it up on the board. 'Does anyone know what these letters stand for? A-D-D? Attention deficit disorder. That's what Luke has, so his behavior problems are not his fault.'"

Luke paused. "There are still some losers who call me that, ADD Boy."

Sierra made a sudden guess.

"Mitch. When you were fighting last week. *That's* what he called you."

Luke didn't answer, but Sierra knew she had guessed right.

"I hate your third-grade teacher, too," Sierra whispered. "I hate all of them. Her, and Mrs. Nolan, and the one who couldn't pronounce Julio's name."

"But which of *your* teachers do *you* hate the most?" Luke asked.

"I hate Ms. Lin," she offered.

"Doesn't count. Everybody hates Lintbag. Probably her own parents hate her."

She might as well confess. "Okay, I lose. I never hated any of them."

"Suck-up. Ass kisser," Luke said, but not in a mean way, more in a friendly, almost flirty way.

If Em had been here in suspension—but how far away Sierra's former friends seemed right now—Em would have said, "Luke Bishop likes you."

23

At lunchtime, with Mrs. Saunders out for the day and Ms. Lin alone in the office, the four suspendees were allowed to walk to the cafeteria to buy lunch unescorted.

"I told Sandy to keep an eye on you," Ms. Lin told them. "So I don't want to hear about any funny business."

Little did Ms. Lin know that all the funny business had already happened during the five minutes that she was out of the office a few hours ago. The *Denver Post* might very well not print Ms. Lin's letter to the editor—the only one of Sierra's that had been published was about the importance of bike safety. But then again, it very well might.

If only Sierra hadn't sent it!

But Ms. Lin deserved it, Sierra kept telling herself.

And either way, it couldn't be unsent.

As the four of them entered the cafeteria, Sierra

wondered if Colin would come over to talk to her again. It might be awkward without Mrs. Saunders there to monitor the conversation so that Luke didn't say anything inappropriate, like *Coming to talk to your girlfriend?*

On the one hand, if Luke said that and Colin heard it, it might give Colin the appealing idea that Sierra *should* be his girlfriend. On the other hand, it might scare him off instead. Was it better if a boy gradually became your boyfriend without even realizing it, so that by the time he did realize what was going on, it was already too late? Her mother had made it sound that way with her father: he came to her play with a friend, laughed at the wrong time, and then the next thing he knew they were married.

Colin looked up from his seat by the window. He didn't give her a full-fledged wave, but he held his hand up in greeting and gave her a big smile.

Back in the suspension room, eating her hot dog, crinkle fries, and iceberg lettuce with Thousand Island dressing, Sierra thought about Colin's smile. And she thought about it some more as she turned the pages of Anne Frank's diary.

She had expected the book to be mainly about how terrible the Holocaust was, how horrible it was to be Jewish in a country under Nazi occupation. But it wasn't that way at all. It was mainly about Anne's intense feelings as a teenager—her quarrels with her mother, her crush on Peter, who was living in hiding with her. If Anne Frank were alive and going to Longwood Middle School, Sierra could have talked to her about Colin, and Anne would have understood completely.

Sierra was lost so deeply in Anne's life that it was a few seconds before she realized that she could hear Mr. Besser's voice, talking to Ms. Lin. Even in one-on-one conversations, his voice projected as if the only style of speech he had was addressing the entire student body at an assembly.

". . . Attorney for the district," he was saying. "Tomorrow morning at ten."

"Stephen was in this morning while you were out," Ms. Lin said.

Mr. Lydgate's first name was Stephen.

"He's worried that there may be a problem with the choir trip to the Springs."

"What kind of problem?" Mr. Besser asked.

Sierra crept out of her seat and flattened herself against the hallway just beyond the rear entrance to the main office so that she could hear better. From where she had positioned herself she could see Mr. Besser but not Ms. Lin.

"If the Shepard girl isn't allowed to go on the trip," Ms. Lin said, "it's going to spoil the balance of the voices. Something like that."

"She *can't* go. I told him that already. First, she's suspended, and that's what suspension *means*: no participation in any school activities during the suspension period—sports, theater, choir, anything. Second, Friday is the day of the hearing."

"Well, he said he's coming to talk with you once school is dismissed."

Mr. Besser turned to leave. His jaw was twitching in an irritated way.

"Oh, and he said that one of the choir members is trying to get the others to refuse to go if Sierra can't go," Ms. Lin continued. "Organizing some kind of a boycott."

Was it Colin? *Please, please, please let it be Colin.* One thing Sierra knew for sure: it wasn't Celeste.

Mr. Besser stopped and whirled around.

"Which member? When do they rehearse? I'll go talk to them myself and put a stop to this nonsense."

Sierra jumped as his office door shut, too loudly, but she managed not to give herself away. She slipped back to the suspension room undetected just as the closing bell sounded for the day.

24

There were no reporters waiting in the parking lot. Even though Sierra was relieved not to have to see her sad self on TV again, she felt a pang of disappointment, almost irritation. So that was it for her fifteen minutes of fame. She could be expelled without anybody knowing or caring, supplanted by the story of how the city hadn't sent out enough snow plows because of budget cuts.

She saw their Volvo and slid into the front seat. Her mother's face was lit with the same kind of excitement as when she was in the middle of writing a play.

"What?" Sierra asked.

"Don't tell your father." Her mother backed out of her parking space into the long line of cars waiting to crawl into the exit lane. "We're just going to stop by Beautiful Mountain so you can meet the principal and see what you think."

"But I already said I don't want to change schools, and Daddy doesn't want me to change, either."

"That's why we're not going to mention this to him just yet. Honey, I visited there this morning, did a school tour, sat in on an art class. I think you're going to love it."

"I don't want to change schools," Sierra repeated.

"Honey?" Her mother was so intent on their conversation that she cut off another car as she finally pushed her way out of the parking lot. "Honey, you may have to change schools whether you want to or not."

Hearing her mother say that, her own mother, in such a matter-of-fact tone, scared Sierra more than anything that had happened yet.

"But Daddy—"

"Your father doesn't win every case. No lawyer does. I'm just saying that you have options. That's all. And, I might add, very attractive options."

Beautiful Mountain was on the edge of town, in a strikingly pretty setting, situated against protected mountain open space, with its network of inviting hiking trails. Instead of one large building, like Longwood Middle School, there was a cluster of smaller buildings, like cozy cottages tucked in the woods. The littleness of the buildings made it look like an elementary school, or even a preschool, in Sierra's opinion.

"How many grades go here?" she asked.

"There's an elementary school, a middle school, and a high school, all on one campus."

"Campus" sounded like a college, but it was hardly a college.

"That's one of the things I find most appealing about it," her mother said as she parked the car in the empty visitor lot. "If you're ready for more advanced classes in any subject area, which I'm sure you are, you can just step into the next building."

"Where is everybody?" Sierra asked.

"Well, school is out for the day, of course. But there are only a hundred and thirty students in all twelve grades."

"So they can't have very many classes to pick from," Sierra pointed out. "I bet they don't have any advanced classes at all. Do they have calculus? Or . . ." She tried to think of some other hard, impressive course.

"You haven't even walked in the door yet," her mother replied.

Outside the main building—the only way Sierra could tell it was the main building was by the small sign bearing the word OFFICE—two older boys with longish hair stood loitering.

"They need haircuts," Sierra said.

"Oh, some kids just want to be a little different. They don't want to cross every *t* and dot every *i*."

Sierra liked crossing *t*'s and dotting *i*'s.

Or she used to.

Inside the main building, the walls were filled with student artwork—vividly colored self-portraits. Full-grown trees in terra-cotta pots stretched toward the ceiling sky-light.

The secretary in the front office was a young woman who looked barely old enough to be out of college, dressed in blue jeans and a loose, embroidered cotton top. Her frizzy hair was even wilder than Sierra's mother's.

"Nice to see you again," the secretary said. "I'll let Jackie know you and your daughter are here."

Jackie turned out to be the principal, who at least had on a dress rather than jeans, but a flowing African-patterned dress that didn't seem to Sierra like what a principal would wear.

"Welcome to Beautiful Mountain, Sierra," Jackie said with a warm, crinkly smile. Jackie's close-cropped gray hair set off her long, dangling earrings.

Does she know about me? Does she know what happened to me?

"Your mother told me that you love the arts," Jackie said. "And that you're a strong student leader at Long-wood Middle School."

Sierra didn't know if she was a *strong* student leader. "I'm in Leadership Club."

"Well, here we love students who take initiative," Jackie said. "We value student ideas enormously. But one difference you'll find at Beautiful Mountain is that, while we have a lot of student leaders, we don't have many student followers." She laughed in a friendly way.

Then her tone changed. "I'm sorry for what you're

going through right now," she said softly. "It must be very difficult."

Sierra was torn between gratitude for Jackie's genuine-sounding sympathy and a desire, however paradoxical, to defend her school.

"Don't you have rules here?" she asked. The question came out sounding more hostile than she had intended.

"Of course we do. Human beings couldn't live together without rules. Our students themselves play a big role in shaping those rules."

Jackie put her arm around Sierra's shoulders. It might have felt presumptuous or intrusive, but it didn't.

"But, Sierra, no student would ever get expelled from Beautiful Mountain for trying to do the right thing. I can promise you that."

Even as her eyes pricked with tears, Sierra tried to defend Mr. Besser one more time. It was strange, but defending Mr. Besser was almost like defending her father, too. They both thought Longwood Middle School was vastly better than some "progressive" alternative.

"So students can bring knives to school here and nothing happens?"

"Nothing happens," Jackie said gently, "if someone brings a knife to school by mistake."

As Jackie led Sierra and her mother on a mini-tour of Beautiful Mountain, Sierra noticed that the classrooms were ridiculously small—ten desks!—and that the library for the entire school had hardly more books in it than

Sierra's book-crammed house. Yes, there was art everywhere, but the Longwood Middle School art teacher was terrific, too—Sierra thought again of her poor, abandoned pot. And would any choir from Beautiful Mountain be chosen from schools all around the state to perform at the big music educators' convention?

But part of Sierra remembered the frizzy-haired secretary greeting her with a friendly "Hey."

Part of Sierra remembered the warmth of Jackie's comforting arm around her shoulders.

"So what did you think?" her mother asked her as they got in the car to drive away.

Sierra gazed out the car window at the falling January darkness. "It was okay."

25

Halfway through Tuesday morning, Sierra had to admit it: she missed Luke Bishop. She read Anne Frank while Julio and Brad played on their Game Boys, careful to hold them hidden on their laps under the table. The three of them had no interaction aside from an initial hello as the boys wandered in, separately, a few minutes after the tardy bell.

Mrs. Saunders escorted them to lunch at the start of 4A.

"Did your son's wisdom teeth surgery turn out okay?" Sierra asked her.

"Aren't you sweet to ask," Mrs. Saunders said. "It was fine, though I think he's already tired of Jello and vanilla pudding."

Julio followed behind them, saying nothing; Brad had brought his lunch from home. They both had three-day suspensions, so their suspensions would end tomorrow.

Only Sierra had done something so unforgivable that her suspension would last forever.

Today Colin was obviously scanning the lunch line, looking for her. As soon as she picked up her tray of macaroni-and-beef casserole, canned corn, canned pears, and small carton of milk, he came over to talk to her.

"Did you hear?" he asked, his gray eyes fastened on hers.

"Is it about the choir trip?"

"Three of us told Mr. Lydgate that we won't go if you can't go, and if we don't go, there's no way the choir can perform. Counting you, that's half the choir."

Sierra looked down at her tray, abashed. Colin was her knight in shining armor—a soft-spoken, not very tall knight whose long-tapered fingers had a slight tremor—charging off to the Crusades with her banner flying above him.

"I heard Besser is furious," Colin continued. "Mr. Lydgate told us Besser wants to come talk to us at our rehearsal on Thursday morning, the last rehearsal before the trip, if there is a trip, to convince us to go."

"What about Mr. Lydgate? Is he upset, too?"

"He's one of the teachers who signed the petition. He hates zero tolerance. So I think he's jazzed that we're doing this. But he'll be bummed if the choir doesn't go, because it's this huge feather in his cap as a music teacher if we do go. So I think he's hoping that Besser will back down so you can go and we all can go. But if Besser doesn't back down, I think he hopes we'll give in and end the boycott."

Sierra could hardly make herself ask the next thrilling question, but she did.

"*Will* you back down?" She met Colin's earnest gaze, wishing her eyes were wide and intense like his.

"Not a chance."

Mrs. Saunders, who had been standing a short distance away, interrupted. "We need to be getting back, Sierra."

"Who else is doing the boycott with you?" Sierra had to ask before leaving the cafeteria.

"Jeremy and Alicia."

Sierra would have bet a million dollars, if she had a million dollars, that it wouldn't be Celeste.

"Wow. Thanks," Sierra said.

"You don't need to thank me," Colin said.

Her heart sang as she floated back to the suspension room.

Will you back down?

Not a chance.

It was another afternoon without reporters, further proof that Sierra's imminent expulsion was yesterday's news. It was another afternoon without Em, Lexi, and Celeste, too: they all had a Leadership Club meeting after school.

Her father was home when she and her mother came in from the garage to the kitchen. Sometimes, especially after a big case ended, he worked from home. Right now he had his laptop set up on the kitchen table, catching up on e-mail as he listened to classical music on the public radio station.

He stood up to kiss Sierra's mother on the mouth and to give Sierra a quick hard hug. Sierra hung up her coat and dropped down into the chair next to him as her mother put on the kettle for tea.

"How's my brave girl? Still sticking it out with the cretins and the criminals?"

"Gerald!" her mother chided him. "Just because kids are assigned to an in-school suspension doesn't mean that they're dumb or bad. You of all people should know that right now."

"I wasn't talking about the kids in suspension," he said. "I was talking about the school administrators who put them there."

He laughed, but Sierra's mother didn't laugh with him.

"I don't even like the word 'cretin.' It's derogatory. It's hurtful to people who have developmental challenges."

"Now, don't go all politically correct on me," he said, his tone affectionate, like Luke's yesterday, calling Sierra a suck-up and an ass kisser.

The phone rang. No one bothered to get up to answer it. It was probably just some reporter who still hadn't given up on the same-old, same-old story.

"You have reached the Shepard residence," said her

mother's voice on the tape. "Please leave a message at the tone."

After the beep, a woman's voice spoke.

"This is Jackie DuChamp at Beautiful Mountain. I just want to thank you and Sierra for taking the time to stop by yesterday, and see if you had any further questions I could answer for you."

Halfway through the message, Sierra's father stood up from his chair and was over by the phone mounted on the far wall, his eyes narrow with anger. Sierra hoped he wouldn't pick up the phone and tell Jackie what he thought about artsy-fartsy schools for fruits and nuts who didn't know how to think.

He let the message finish. Then he turned his furious gaze on Sierra's mother.

"What was that?"

Sierra was impressed as her mother raised her chin and kept her own gaze steady. "I told you I wanted to stop by just to take a look."

"And *I* told *you* to forget about it. I'm not having my daughter throw away a first-class education at the most rigorous school in the district for some touchy-feely hippie nonsense."

Now her mother's eyes flashed with her own anger. "For your information, Gerald, when I visited Beautiful Mountain I came away very impressed. There is more creativity in one single classroom in that school than in all of Longwood Middle School put together."

"Creativity?" Her father made it sound like a dirty word. "You want me to pay twenty thousand dollars a year for creativity? Call me strange, call me old-fashioned, but I want Sierra to go to a school where she actually learns something."

"And what is she learning where she is now? Obey every rule, however idiotic, however inane, and if you break a rule in complete and total innocence, you may have your life destroyed? That's what you want her to learn?"

Sierra had never seen her parents fight this way before. She shrank back in her chair, willing herself to disappear.

"No one's *life* is going to be *destroyed*," her father said. "Sierra is going to learn that you can fight for your rights. Do you want her to learn that if your rights are threatened, you just run away to the happy, feel-good flower children and make beaded necklaces and macramé sandals all day?"

"Do you know any way to respond to other people's ideas and opinions without being insulting and demeaning?" her mother shot back.

"Not if the ideas are ludicrous, I don't."

"So my ideas are ludicrous?"

Sierra's father pounded the palm of his open hand against his forehead; he was obviously trying to pull himself together.

"No," he said. "I don't think your ideas are ludicrous.

But this one—all right, you're making me say it—this one is."

"Because this school values creativity. Well, guess what? You married someone who is creative. You married a playwright."

Don't, Sierra beamed the word toward her father. But she was powerless to stop him.

"A playwright who is pretty darned lucky to be married to an attorney. To someone who actually makes money. Uncreative as that is, it does come in handy every once in a while. Like when there's the small matter of a mortgage to pay. Or to get a few uncreative things like heat, and electricity, and running water. How far do you think you'd get with your creative hobby if it weren't for your uncreative husband—"

He broke off midsentence, but it was too late. His wife was covering her mouth as if she might be sick.

"Look, I didn't mean it that way. I respect your work, you know I do."

She cut him off. "My hobby. My pitiful plays that never get produced and that don't make any money. You respect them."

"Honey."

He came over to where she was sitting and stooped down to try to put his arm around her shaking shoulders.

"Get away from me. Don't touch me."

Stung by her rebuff, he straightened himself to his full standing position, rage rekindled in his eyes.

"None of this would have happened, none of it, if *you* had respected *my* opinions and done what I said."

"What you said," she repeated. "Well, Gerald Edward Shepard, Esquire, after fifteen years a person can get just a wee bit tired of always doing what you say."

She snatched up her purse, which had been draped over the back of one of the kitchen chairs, and fumbled for her car keys. Without even bothering to grab her coat, she fled from the kitchen to the garage. Sierra heard the garage door open and the car engine start.

"She'll be back," her father said, as much to himself as to Sierra.

Sierra buried her face in her hands and began to cry.

26

By six-thirty Sierra's mother still hadn't returned.

Sierra's father knocked on her bedroom door; Sierra was in bed, under the covers, reading Anne Frank, wishing the story could end with Anne Frank still alive.

"I guess we'd better go get some dinner," he said.

The refrigerator was full of food they could have heated up, but her father already had his car keys in his hand.

They drove to an Indian restaurant that had a buffet not just for lunch but for dinner, too. Sierra was glad not to have the awkwardness of waiting to order their food and then waiting for it to arrive. It was easier to talk once they were already settled with plates of sag paneer and aloo gobi for her and lamb curry and tandoori chicken for her father.

"Your mother gets that way," he said. "But she's one of those people who get angry quickly and then get over it quickly. One thing she doesn't do is bear a grudge."

Unlike you?

Sierra pulled off a piece of the soft puffy naan bread and let it dissolve in her mouth.

"How did you and Mom meet?" she asked. She already knew the answer, but wanted to hear how her father would describe it.

He chuckled. "Even back then she was writing plays. So I guess you could say I knew what I was signing up for from minute one. I had never cared for plays, but my roommate dragged me to this one because he had gone out a couple of times with the girl who wrote it. I remember on the way there all I could think was, *I hope it's not a musical.*"

"So you went to one of Mom's plays," Sierra prompted.

He nodded and took a forkful of lamb curry before going on.

"There must have been twenty people in the audience, tops, so it's good we were there to fill two more empty seats."

"Was the play good? Was it funny?"

He chuckled again. "Good? Now, that's a loaded question, honey. No, it wasn't good, if by 'good' you mean ready for Broadway. But you could say it had a big heart. Even the villain in the play—the main character's father, who wasn't going to let his daughter marry the man she loved—turned out to be a decent guy after all. Your mother has a gift for seeing the best in everybody. You have that, too. Me? I have the gift for seeing people as they are."

"You didn't say if it was funny."

"Well, it was supposed to be. Some people in the audience were laughing at some of the better lines, but with such a small audience, it's hard."

"So did *you* laugh?"

"Well, there was one spot—the actor had just delivered a line that you could tell he thought was pretty hilarious. And then, I don't think anyone else saw it, but I could see that he realized that his fly was partway open, and he tried to do it up casually so no one would see. I pretty much lost it there, laughing. But it was good for the performance. It loosened up the rest of the audience, and then they were more willing to laugh at whatever happened next. The contagion effect."

Sierra ripped off another piece of bread and rolled it into a small hard ball between her fingers.

"Does Mom know? That you didn't really think her play was funny, but that you just thought it was funny that one of the actors had his pants unzipped?"

"Of course not. Sierra, I would never do or say anything, intentionally, to hurt you or your mother. You understand that? That hobby stuff I said before—I never would have said that if I hadn't been provoked."

He took a long swig from his glass of water.

"Look. Your mother had no right to go traipsing over

to look at that school, not after I had expressly said I didn't want her doing that."

Sierra waited to see if he would ask her what *she* thought of Beautiful Mountain. If he did, she wasn't sure what she would say. But he didn't.

"Honey, you're too smart for a place like that. You may see the good in people, like your mother, but you have a lot of me in you, too. You'd see through that kumbaya scene in ten minutes, I know you would."

The waiter came by to refill their water glasses, and her father asked for the check.

When they got home, at quarter to eight, Sierra's mother's car was in the garage, but she was already in bed. Or at least she was in the bedroom with the door closed and the lights off.

27

The next morning, Sierra's father had already left for work by the time she came downstairs for breakfast at seven o'clock, but he often went in early, so she didn't know if her parents had made up their quarrel or not. Maybe Sierra would be expelled *and* have a broken home like Luke's, all in one week.

Her mother still looked the same, slim in faded jeans and a turtleneck, with an unbuttoned floral-patterned shirt layered on top, her hair swept back from her face in a scarf.

"There's something in this morning's *Denver Post* that might interest you," her mother said as she set a glass of orange juice in front of Sierra.

She pointed to the first section of the newspaper, folded open to the editorial page.

"Read the editorial 'Zero Tolerance Makes Zero Sense.' Then read the first letter to the editor. It appears that your Ms. Lin has had a change of heart. A very public change of heart."

With her mother expectantly and eagerly looking over her shoulder, Sierra let her eyes scan the paper.

The editors had printed it.

They had actually printed it.

> As the head secretary of Longwood Middle
> School, I am shocked and dismayed by
> the senseless punishment of one of our most
> outstanding students. This is a scandal and
> an outrage.
>
> Susan Lin

"It just goes to show that people can surprise you," Sierra's mother said. "That smug, supercilious smile? That 'I'm just doing my job' defensiveness? Then *she* writes *this*."

Sierra couldn't meet her mother's eyes. She pretended to be busy reading the editorial, which was calling for school weapons policies to be applied "with a modicum of reasonableness and a dollop of common sense."

Her mother filled a blue pottery bowl from a pan on the stove and brought it over to Sierra.

"I made oatmeal today; there's some blueberries to go with it."

Sierra usually liked oatmeal, but today it looked un- usually thick and grayish, as if it would form itself into a hardened slab of cement in the bottom of her stomach.

"I'm not very hungry."

"You will be in an hour if you don't eat up. Are you sure you don't want me to pack you a lunch today? I don't see how you can stand a whole week's worth of cafeteria food."

"It's not so bad."

Not when a trip to the cafeteria meant a chance to see Colin.

"Your Mr. Besser," her mother said as she folded up the newspaper, "is not going to like this one bit."

No, he wasn't.

Ms. Lin wasn't going to like it one bit, either.

Sierra forced herself to swallow down a big mouthful of oatmeal, and then another one.

When Sierra walked into the front office, she felt as if a pulsing neon sign were lit up on her face: GUILTY, GUILTY, GUILTY! She expected a pulsing neon sign to be lit up on Ms. Lin's face: RAGE, RAGE, RAGE! But Ms. Lin was calmly talking on the phone to a parent about the procedures for excusing a student for an orthodontist appointment.

"All of our policies are explained clearly on the school Web site," Ms. Lin said. "You need to check there."

As if it wouldn't take less time to answer the question than to direct someone to the school Web site to get it answered.

"I'd suggest you make every effort to get an after-school appointment," Ms. Lin added. "Even with an excused absence, it can be very difficult for students to make up material."

Would she calmly be offering the same unhelpful help if she had seen the morning's paper? Maybe she didn't get the *Denver Post* at home.

Sierra saw the office copy of the *Post* rolled up in a green plastic bag, lying on the low table in front of the faculty mailboxes.

As she started down the short hallway to the suspension room, Sierra thought: *Now I've actually done something that deserves suspension.* Sending a forged letter to the largest newspaper in the state of Colorado was a far worse offense than using disrespectful language or fighting on school grounds.

She thought of her father's comment to her at the Indian restaurant last night: "I would never have done it if I hadn't been provoked."

Was that an acceptable excuse?

For him or for her?

As always—well, always for the last five days—she was the first one in the suspension room. She couldn't make herself sit down, she couldn't open Anne Frank and resume reading, not when any second Mr. Besser was bound to appear. He would have read the *Denver Post* editorials and letters first thing upon waking, wouldn't he? Given that he was embroiled in a firestorm of terrible publicity?

Undigested oatmeal lay stony in her stomach.

Brad and Julio drifted in. She wished she could tell

them, have them share her apprehension of every sound in the outer office heard through the open door of the suspension room. But out of all the seven billion people on the planet, only Luke Bishop knew what she had done, and even Luke knew only that she had done *something*.

Then, inexplicably, impossibly, Luke was there. Sierra was standing by the door, watching down the hallway for a first glimpse of Mr. Besser, when she saw Luke strolling down the hall toward her, a big grin on his face. She darted inside the room before he could call out a greeting—"Hey, Shep-turd!"—and betray her lurking presence to Ms. Lin.

She felt like hugging him.

"What are *you* doing here?" she asked in a pleased whisper when he walked into the suspension room.

"Just thought I'd drop by to check on the prisoners."

"I didn't think they let us have visitors."

"You're too much," Luke said, shaking his head with mingled amusement and scorn. "You crack me up, really you do."

"Why? What did I say?"

"'I didn't think they let us have visitors.'"

"Then why *are* you here?"

"Why are *you* here? Why are *they* here?" He nodded toward Brad and Julio, hunched over their games.

"You're suspended again?"

"It's been known to happen."

"What did you do this time?"

151

"Stole a car."

Sierra stared at him.

"Give me a break. I dropped the f-bomb in front of a teacher."

"Why?"

"Because I felt like it. Why are you standing by the door like you're a spy or something?"

"Do you read the *Denver Post*?" Sierra asked him in an even lower whisper.

"Every word," Luke said. "I memorize the *Denver Post* in case there's a current events quiz in social studies class, so I can be sure to ace it every time."

"There's a letter to the editor today. About me."

"Well, aren't you the little celebrity. First a TV star, now the star of the *Denver Post*."

Sierra glared at him. She hoped he wasn't going to start that stuff again.

"It says how unfair Mr. Besser is being. It says my suspension is a scandal and an outrage."

Luke gave his trademark sneer. "Big f-bomb deal."

"Luke, the letter was signed by Ms. Lin."

"Get out. That Ms. Lin?"

"Susan Lin, secretary of Longwood Middle School."

Now it was Luke's turn to stare. Now it was Luke's turn not to get it.

Then comprehension broke over his face.

"You," he said. "That day on her computer."

"Yes," Sierra said. "Me."

28

don't think she knows yet," Sierra said. "I don't think she's seen the paper. But I bet he has. Mr. Besser. And when he comes in—"

"It's going to hit the fan," Luke finished the sentence for her.

Julio finally looked up from his game hidden beneath the table. "What are you two whispering about?" Like Sierra previously, he did a double take when he realized that Luke was back so soon after his last suspension had ended.

When neither Luke nor Sierra answered right away, Julio said, "Fine. Whatever," and stared back at his lap again, his hands obviously busy working the controls of his game.

Brad gave them one indifferent glance and said nothing.

"You rock, Sierra Shep-turd," Luke whispered to her.

But what if she did get caught?

HONOR STUDENT FACES CRIMINAL CHARGES FOR FORGERY.

What would her parents say? Her father might react with his own version of Luke's "Go get 'em" response, but her mother would be shocked and disappointed. Maybe her mother would blame her father, and they'd have another huge blowup, and this time her father would tell her mother that he didn't think her plays were even funny, and then they would get divorced.

Would Beautiful Mountain take a convicted criminal as a student?

But how could Mr. Besser catch her? How could anybody ever prove it? Her fingerprints wouldn't still be on Ms. Lin's keyboard after a couple of days of steady typing.

Luke would never give her away. She was as sure of that as she was of anything in the universe, even if she was a good deal less certain about a lot of things than she had been a week ago.

So the only thing that could give her away was her own guilty face, which always showed everything.

Sierra heard the door to the outer office open. Footsteps.

Ms. Lin's voice: "Tom, good morning. It's crazy here already. There's a leak in the gym roof—all that melting snow from the storm last week—and two parents have called about the choir trip, very upset that it might be canceled. Do you want me to—"

Mr. Besser's voice: "Susan."

It was coming now.

"Have you seen the *Denver Post* this morning?"

"No, I haven't had a chance to look at it yet. I don't get the print edition anymore; I just read it online."

"They printed your letter."

"My letter?"

"*If* you had issues with any of my policies, *if* you had problems with how I'm handling the Shepard girl's case, I wish you would have come to talk to me directly before sharing your thoughts with the *Denver Post*'s hundreds of thousands of subscribers. Don't you think I'm going through enough right now, attacked on all sides, and now *this*?"

"But I—"

"Let me finish. Do you know how bad this makes me look? When a member of my staff publicly criticizes my policies?"

Sierra had never heard Mr. Besser sound so angry. During the confrontation with her father, her dad had seemed a lot closer to losing his temper than Mr. Besser had.

"I didn't write any letter!"

"Susan, it's in the paper."

"But—"

"It's in the paper," he repeated.

Sierra heard the door to his inner office slam so hard that both Julio and Brad finally looked up from their video games.

"What was that about?" Brad asked.

Luke's shoulders were shaking with laughter.

Don't give me away! Sierra begged him with her eyes.

"Buttster and Lintbag just had a fight. A brawl, you might call it."

Sierra glared at him. "Stop it! It's not funny!"

Luke's face registered bewilderment. "What do you mean, it's not funny?"

"It's just—not." Not when she had done the terrible thing that caused it. "Stay here," she told Luke.

Soundlessly, she edged her way down the hallway until she was in position to see Ms. Lin at her desk. The green plastic bag from the *Denver Post* lay discarded on the floor.

Mrs. Saunders, who had apparently been in the copy room, returned to the front office.

"Susan, what's wrong?"

"That man!"

"Who?"

"Him. There's an anti-Besser letter in the paper today. Signed by me. But I didn't write it."

Mrs. Saunders walked over to Ms. Lin's desk and read the letter on the open page of the newspaper.

"Oh, no," Mrs. Saunders said. "So that's what he was raising his voice about. But if you didn't write it, who did?"

"Does it matter? How can he have possibly thought I could have written this? Why isn't he on the phone to the *Denver Post* right now reading them the riot act for publishing such a thing without checking first to see if it was a fake?"

Ms. Lin got up from her desk, not even bothering to fold the newspaper but leaving it lying open with "her" letter on display for all to see.

"You know what, Alice? It doesn't matter what he thinks. It doesn't matter one bit. Because as of this minute, I no longer work for him, or for Longwood Middle School. I know he's under a lot of stress these days, we all are, but nobody has ever spoken to me that way—that tone of voice! You can tell him that I've resigned. Or that my tolerance for him is precisely zero."

"Susan. Susan. Listen to me. This is all just a hideous misunderstanding. It can be cleared up. The letter was probably written by one of Sierra's supporters, maybe the kid who made the petition and organized the choir trip boycott. And the paper should have checked unless . . . Was the letter sent by e-mail from a district computer? But I don't see how it could have been; nobody on the faculty or staff would do such a thing. But, Susan, my point is, this will blow over. It isn't worth giving up your job. Not in this economy."

"I will never," Ms. Lin said, "work for that man again. My personal items—will you put them in a box and send them to me?"

Ms. Lin was halfway to the door when she happened to glance down the hallway leading to the suspension room.

"You!" she said to Sierra. "What are *you* doing?"

"I was—I had to—go to the bathroom. And then—I didn't want to walk past you while you were—"

Should she confess? Go to Mr. Besser and tell him who had actually written the letter?

It wouldn't do any good, not now. Ms. Lin would never forgive Mr. Besser.

"If you're going to the bathroom, then go!" Ms. Lin spat at her.

Sierra went. Inside the girls' room she locked herself into an empty stall. Kneeling on the cold floor, she threw up oatmeal and blueberries until all that was left was dry retching.

She wouldn't be able to eat oatmeal ever again.

29

With Ms. Lin gone and Mrs. Saunders left to preside over the office all by herself, there was no one to escort Sierra and Luke to the cafeteria; the other two had brought lunches from home.

"I think you two can be trusted to go alone," Mrs. Saunders said, her eyes meeting Sierra's with a look of kind confidence.

Even though Ms. Lin had let them go by themselves the other day, when she had no choice, it was hard to imagine her ever uttering such a sentence.

But Ms. Lin would have been correct in her belief that Sierra and Luke couldn't be trusted.

It was one of those warm end-of-January days. Last week's snow was already melting off the lawns, and kids were outdoors for lunch recess without bothering with jackets.

"We could go outside for a while," Luke said. "She's not going to notice when we come back."

"We'd better not," Sierra said. "She's been so nice." She wasn't going to betray Mrs. Saunders, especially now, after what she had done to Ms. Lin and how it had turned out.

Colin waved to her but didn't come over to give her any boycott bulletins. Then, as she was about to head out with her tray, he appeared in front of her, his face a bit wary. Probably he didn't want to be drawn into conversation with Luke.

"Jolene joined us, too. So the trip's definitely off unless Besser can talk the rest of them out of it at rehearsal tomorrow morning. Lydgate would go with seven, but he can't possibly go with fewer than that."

"La-la-la-la-la-la!" Luke sang in a loud, rude falsetto. "Sounds to me like you'll all be doing the world a big fat favor not to inflict your singing on it."

"Just ignore him," Sierra said to Colin. Was Luke making fun of Colin for being a boy in choir, as if choir were more of a girl thing? Luke shouldn't talk: he didn't do *anything* except get in fights and cuss in front of teachers.

She tried to give Colin a smile that was more than just a thank-you-for-being-my-hero smile; she wanted it to be a please-like-me-as-much-as-I-like-you smile. But she wasn't able to give him her best smile in front of Luke.

"Why are you so mean to everybody?" she asked Luke as they carried their trays down the hall to the office.

"I'm not mean to everybody. Just to *almost* everybody."

"Who *aren't* you mean to?"

"I'm not mean to you."

"Anymore. Except you still call me Shep-turd. You said you wouldn't, but you still do."

"Aw, it's kind of a—what do you call it?—a pet name. Like Snookums."

"Snookums?"

"Yeah. Sierra Snookums Shep-turd. I like it."

She was giggling as they entered the office but stopped when she saw Mr. Besser deep in conversation with Mrs. Saunders. He shot Sierra a piercing look that made her sure that he knew. He might not be ready to confront her yet, but he knew.

Or maybe that was just her guilt speaking?

It didn't help that she felt a blush rising up from her chest to her neck to her face.

That afternoon, she finished reading the last pages of Anne Frank's diary. When she read the afterword, telling how Anne had died at Auschwitz, her eyes stung with tears. She would never complain about anything in her life ever again, not even if she was expelled or sentenced to a juvenile detention center for forgery. Nothing that happened to her could be as wrong and terrible as what had happened to Anne Frank.

"You're crying over a book?" Luke asked her.

Sierra nodded. She held it up so he could see the cover. "Didn't you ever cry over a book? Or a movie?"

"Nope. It makes me mad when people try to make me cry. I won't give them the satisfaction. Never would."

"Even when you were little?"

"Even when I was little. All right, no. I did cry when Bambi's mother died. But my dad said big boys don't cry, so I stopped."

"How old were you?"

"Three? Or four?"

Sierra felt a pang of sadness for little boy Luke, not even allowed to cry over Bambi's mother.

"But, anyway," she said, "with Anne Frank, it's not like Anne is trying to make anybody cry. You cry because of what *happened* to Anne, and that's just a fact."

She paused.

"How long is your suspension this time?"

"Three days."

Sierra didn't think she should tell Luke that she was glad he had been suspended again. She didn't want to give him the wrong idea.

But she was glad. She really was.

After school the Channel 9 van was there, but no reporters from any other stations.

"Sierra!"

The blond reporter felt like an old friend now.

Sierra hadn't realized how much she had missed the daily TV interviews until she felt the camera trained on her face once more to catch her every fleeting expression.

The world did care what happened to her.

"Sierra, the expulsion hearing is on Friday. That's just two days away. What do you think the superintendent will rule in your case?"

"I think I'll get to stay."

Actually, she had no idea, but she knew that was what her father would want her to say.

"Even though school policy explicitly states that any possession of any weapon on school grounds for any reason means automatic expulsion?"

Sierra nodded. "It just doesn't make sense to expel someone for a mistake."

Blah, blah, blah, blah, blah.

"There have been some voices raised in your support over the last few days. Eight teachers signed the school petition protesting the principal's decision. And just this morning, in the *Denver Post*, a member of the school staff wrote a letter sharply critical of the principal's actions."

Sierra tried to keep her cheeks from flushing as they had before.

Out of the corner of her eye she caught a glimpse of Colin leaving the school. Maybe he would come over and rescue her yet again by telling the blond reporter about the choir trip boycott.

Until then, she had to make some reply.

"I think it's great that people are speaking out."

Colin was with someone, a girl who looked like Celeste. It *was* Celeste.

Maybe he was trying to talk her into joining the boy-cott, speaking softly in his intense, persuasive way. Even smug, self-righteous Celeste wouldn't be able to hold out against an appeal made in Colin's low voice, the direct gaze of Colin's gray eyes.

They were coming down the front steps of the school.

They were still talking.

He was holding her hand.

30

Sierra had no idea what else the blond reporter asked or what else she replied.

Colin and Celeste came closer. They had stopped to watch her being interviewed.

Five minutes ago Sierra would have been glad to have Celeste see her back in the media spotlight. Celeste might not think Sierra had suffered an outrageous injustice, but obviously 9NEWS did.

Now she didn't care anymore if she was expelled. She *wanted* to be expelled, and the sooner the better, so that she would never have to spend another minute of her life at Longwood Middle School. Whatever her father said about fruits and nuts, she was going to transfer to Beautiful Mountain. She would tell her mother to call them tomorrow. Or they could stop by the school on the way home to tell Jackie in person.

Colin and *Celeste*?

Celeste and *Colin*?

A sharp knife of heartbreak and humiliation—much sharper than her mother's apple-cutting knife—stabbed itself into Sierra's heart.

"I know it's tough," she heard the reporter say. "Just remember, Sierra, you have a lot of supporters around the state of Colorado who are out there cheering for you."

The interview was over.

Colin and Celeste had walked on. At Celeste's urging? Did Celeste suspect Sierra's crush on Colin? Sierra had taken such pains to hide her feelings from Celeste. If Celeste had known, would it have made any difference? Or would it only have made this moment that much more excruciating?

Sierra stumbled toward her mother's car.

"What is it? What happened?"

Sitting beside her mother in the front seat, Sierra leaned her head against the glass of the window, unable to let her mother's worried eyes probe her face.

"What did they do to you? Was it Mr. Besser? Or one of the other kids in suspension? Tell me. You have to tell me, or I'm going to march into the office right now and find out myself."

"Nothing happened!"

"What do you mean, nothing happened? This is cruel, what they're doing to you, cruel. I'm going in there and telling Mr. Besser that enough is enough."

"No! Don't go in there. There's nothing anyone can do, or Daddy would have already done it."

"Actually, your father called me just now, and told me there have been some developments, there *is* something he can do. But I'm not willing to wait until that charade of a hearing. Do you want to wait here, or do you want to come in with me?"

Her mother had already unbuckled her seatbelt.

"Mom. This. Has. Nothing. To. Do. With. That."

"Then what does it . . . Oh." Her mother sighed and said just one word: "Colin."

Sierra didn't bother to tell her mother that she was right.

"Okay, honey, let's just go, then." Her mother re-buckled her seatbelt and turned the key in the ignition. "Do you want to stop for ice cream on the way home?"

"Ice cream?"

"It actually does help. In these situations. Trust me on this one."

"You *knew*?" Sierra shrieked at Em, who was sitting next to her on her bed.

Em clapped her hands over her ears. Cornflake jumped off Sierra's lap and streaked away.

As soon as they had gotten home from the ice cream parlor, Sierra had called Em: "It's something terrible. Can you come over right now?"

Ten minutes later, Em was there, perched on Sierra's bed behind Sierra's closed door. But when Sierra blurted out, "Colin likes Celeste," Em's face failed to register the shock Sierra had expected.

"You knew, and you didn't tell me? You just let me keep on liking him? And talking about him? And all the while—"

"It wasn't like that. I didn't know until fifth period today. I sort of suspected yesterday, but it wasn't until—"

"What made you suspect yesterday?"

It was sick, but she couldn't help herself, she had to hear Em tell her, with Em's famous attention to every tiny detail.

"Okay. So in French class? Before Madame Moline began? They were talking together. You know how she sits on the other side of him from where you sit. They were talking about you."

"About me." Sierra swallowed hard. "Who said something first?"

"Colin."

Oh, Colin . . .

"He said to Celeste, 'I think you should join the boycott.'"

"How did he look when he said it?"

Not that she needed to ask. Em would tell her anyway.

"His voice was really quiet and intense, you know how he is, like he's soooo serious, like what he's saying matters to him soooo much."

Yes, Sierra knew exactly how Colin was.

"And she said, 'But we all worked so hard to get this. We *earned* this.' And he said, 'Sierra earned it, too.'"

Was it possible to die of love? Of love for a boy who was holding the hand of your friend?

"And she said, 'I feel terrible about Sierra, too.'"

Did she feel so terrible? If she did, Sierra certainly hadn't noticed it.

"But then she said, 'Colin, I think it's great what you're trying to do for Sierra, but I'm sorry, this trip, it just means so much to me to get to go, and now it's all *ruined*.'"

Sierra helped out with the story, even though she hadn't been there. "And then she had tears in her eyes, actual tears, not making her eyes look red and puffy, but making them look big and shiny, and there was one tear glistening in her eyelashes."

"You're good," Em said admiringly to Sierra. "You really are good. Yes! And then he reached over . . ."

Could Sierra stand to hear the rest?

"And he put his hand on hers. Sort of like, to comfort her. And he said, 'I know it's disappointing. I'm disappointed, too.'"

"And then he forgot to take his hand away," Sierra interjected.

"Yeah. He kind of left it there. And he said, 'I wish I could convince you. Are you going to be around after school today?' And she nodded and said, and her voice was kind of shaky, 'I could meet you by the tree.'"

The huge oak tree on the school's front lawn was the school's designated meeting place.

"And then Madame Moline said, '*Bonjour, mes enfants!*' And class began."

"So what about today? What happened today?"

"When they came into French class—" Em began.

"He was holding her hand," Sierra finished the sentence.

"Yeah."

"But at lunch today, during 4A, he told me Jolene had joined the boycott," Sierra said. "He didn't say Celeste had joined it."

"Maybe he's still trying to talk her into it, and now she'll join because she likes Colin so much."

"When she wouldn't do it for me," Sierra said. Her mouth tasted of bitterness, as if she had swallowed a huge mouthful of unripe plum.

"Well," she made herself say, "Colin has a right to like anybody he wants. If he wants to like Celeste, he has a right to like Celeste. And it wasn't as if I ever told Celeste I liked Colin. So she has a right to like Colin, too."

She supposed that was even true. But right now she was too tired—too profoundly weary and heartsick—to care.

Except that she did care.

Oh, Colin!

31

Sierra was in bed for the night, half asleep, when her father got home. It wasn't that late, a bit past nine o'clock, but she was too drained from her day to start a new book or watch anything on TV. She didn't even want to watch herself on TV. No, she *especially* didn't want to watch herself on TV.

A knock came on her bedroom door, not her mother's gentle tap but the vigorous rap of more assertive knuckles.

"Come in," she called faintly.

He had already pushed the door open. "Are you awake?"

She heard suppressed excitement in his voice. That's right—her mother had said there were some "developments," as if Sierra cared about any "developments" in a world where Colin liked Celeste.

"Yes," Sierra told him. "I'm still awake."

"Come on down to the family room. There's something I want to tell you and your mother."

Sierra pulled on the ratty terry-cloth bathrobe that she wouldn't let her mother throw away and scuffed her feet into the huge bunny slippers Lexi had given her for Christmas. Once downstairs, she settled herself sideways on the couch, her legs stretched out with her feet on her mother's lap and Cornflake lying heavy against her tense stomach. The occasion felt strangely solemn—to be summoned from her bed for an announcement so important that it couldn't keep till morning.

"What is it?" she asked her father. "What happened?"

"One thing I have down at the law firm," he began, "is a truly crackerjack staff. I mean, top-notch. I want them to do something today, it's done *yesterday*."

She should have known he wouldn't rush whatever he had to say.

"So I asked Quincy, our research whiz, to do a little checking. Just to see if he could find anything interesting."

"Find anything interesting about what?"

"About a special friend of yours and mine. Mr. Thomas Alford Besser."

"Like what kind of thing?"

"Well, here's an example. I myself think it's very interesting that a Mr. Thomas Alford Besser has on his record a DUI."

Sierra must have looked blank, because her father

stopped to explain, emphasizing each word with careful deliberation.

"Driving under the influence. Yes, the champion of zero tolerance for other people appears to have quite a high level of tolerance when it comes to himself. When the cop pulled him over, his blood alcohol level was three times the legal limit. Not twice. Three times. I don't know about you, but I happen to find that interesting. Downright fascinating."

"But . . ." Sierra's mother hesitated, as if unwilling to say anything that would mar her husband's evident enjoyment of the moment. "A lot of people have infractions when they're young. Maybe I shouldn't say this in front of Sierra—and, Sierra, honey, I never, ever want you to do this when you're old enough to drive—but once when I was in college I drove home from a party where I had been drinking too much, and I careened into a curb so hard I flattened my tire. It was sheer luck that I wasn't pulled over, or worse, didn't hit somebody."

Sierra's father brushed his wife's story away with a wave of his hand.

"Do you want to know when Mr. Thomas Alford Besser had his DUI? Was it after a fraternity party when he was nineteen? No, it was not. It was two months ago. November twenty-ninth, to be precise."

"This past November?" Sierra tried to wrap her mind around the date.

"Why wasn't it in the papers?" her mother asked.

"It happened back in Massachusetts, where he was visiting his parents for Thanksgiving. Lucky for him. Or, should I say, lucky for him until I gave Quincy that little research assignment. Somehow I don't think it's going to look so good when it's in the papers here—the principal who is all set to expel a twelve-year-old girl for bringing an apple knife to school by mistake was arrested for getting behind the wheel of a car with blood alcohol levels three times the legal limit? I think Mr. Thomas Alford Besser may find himself out of a job faster than you can spell the word 'hypocrite.'"

Sierra pulled the frayed belt on her bathrobe to tighten it. "So what are you going to do?"

"Well, given that reporters from half a dozen major newspapers have called our house a total of twenty or more times over the course of the past week, I imagine I could find one or two who might think this information, shall we say, relevant to the case at hand."

The look on his face was the same Sierra had seen on Cornflake as the cat crouched, waiting to pounce on a fake mouse at the end of a cat tease toy, gathering concentration for the kill, but in no hurry to pounce right away.

"So that is one option," her father said.

He was standing facing the couch where Sierra and her mother were sitting, as if he were in the courtroom addressing the jury.

"Or," he said, "I suppose I could stop by Longwood

Middle School tomorrow. I know Tom has an open-door policy, welcoming parents to come in even without an appointment when they have a concern. So I could drop by to see if my possession of this information might influence his desire to proceed with the expulsion hearing, or consider other alternatives."

"Are you talking about blackmail?" Sierra's mother asked.

"That's not the way I would put it. I'd prefer to call it a mutually advantageous arrangement for all parties concerned. I have information that he'd rather not have revealed. I also have a daughter I'd rather not have expelled. So we work something out."

"But that *is* blackmail," Sierra's mother said.

Sierra's father made no reply. Instead, he resumed his argument.

"Then there's a third option. I might save this interesting tidbit of information for one more day. And then I might mention it on Friday, during the course of a certain public hearing where I think our friendly reporters will also be present with some friendly cameramen as well. I think option three might make for some memorable footage, wouldn't you say?"

Sierra's mother hugged Sierra's feet; she seemed to be seeking to comfort herself as much as to comfort Sierra.

Finally she spoke. "Gerald, I don't—"

"You don't what?"

"I don't think . . ."

She didn't finish her sentence.

"Now don't go getting all bighearted and oh-poor-Tom-Besser on me. I warned him. You heard me, both of you. I've been in this business a long, long time, and everyone should know by now that it's not a good idea to mess with Gerald Shepard. And it's an even worse idea to mess with his kid. And if you do, you shouldn't be surprised if you end up getting squished like a bug."

Sierra would never have guessed that she could feel sorry for Mr. Besser, but right now she did. All right, he had done something terrible, more than one thing that was terrible.

But she had done something terrible, too.

32

Sierra couldn't sleep. She always had trouble sleeping if she stayed up too late, as if once the appropriate time for falling asleep had passed, that was it, and she wouldn't get another chance at sleep until another proper bedtime rolled around. Now, in addition, she heard inside her head the measured tones of her father's voice, more menacing than if he had exploded in rage.

She couldn't remember a single time that he had ever punished her for anything when she was little, that he had ever so much as scolded her. But even when she was little, she had somehow known that disobeying her father wasn't an option. She hadn't thought, *Oh, I should put my toys back in the toy chest because Daddy will be mad if I don't.* It had truly never occurred to her that refusing to do what he said existed as a possibility.

Sierra turned her pillow over, glad of its coolness against her flushed cheek. She had heard a simile a couple of weeks ago: "cool as the other side of the pillow."

Whoever had made up that simile must have known what it was to be lying awake at 12:30 a.m., trying out the other side of the pillow to see if you might feel a bit drowsier if you laid your face against it.

Mr. Besser was a hypocrite.

He deserved to have his DUI exposed on TV.

He deserved to be squished like a bug.

Sierra just didn't want to be there when it happened. Whereas her father did, and he wanted to be the one who made it happen.

What about Ms. Lin? Hadn't Sierra squished her like a bug? She hadn't meant for her spur-of-the-moment e-mail to have such far-reaching consequences. She hadn't meant for Ms. Lin to lose her job. Not that Ms. Lin had lost her job exactly; she had been the one who had quit. No one had made her quit. But she had felt too affronted by Mr. Besser's scolding to stay.

Ms. Lin was mean.

She had a bug-squishing personality of her own, except that instead of squishing bugs, she squished middle school kids.

But what Sierra had done was unforgivable. What Sierra had done had changed Ms. Lin's life forever.

The other side of the pillow was no longer cool. Sierra flipped the pillow over again, but the *other* other side hadn't had time to cool back down again. Now both sides of the pillow were hot, and she felt sticky and sweaty inside her nightgown. The green-lit numerals on the clock beside her bed read 12:45.

And Colin. What was the point of his petition and his boycott? It obviously wasn't to declare his love for her.

How could Colin like Celeste?

And what about the choir trip? Would it be ruined? It would serve Celeste right if it was, for caring more about a spoiled class trip than she did about an expelled ex-friend.

But what about the others, who had worked so hard for so many months, all those early mornings of practice after practice since September?

And Mr. Lydgate was so nice. He was young for a teacher, maybe in his late twenties. Having his students picked to perform at the music convention was probably the best thing that had ever happened to him as a middle school music teacher.

Mr. Lydgate deserved to get to go to Colorado Springs with his choir, the choir he was so proud of, and conduct them as they performed on the big stage.

What did Sierra deserve for what she had done to Ms. Lin?

And Luke Bishop, suspended twice within a week: what did Luke deserve?

But before Sierra could finish answering her questions about Mr. Besser, and Ms. Lin, and Celeste, and Colin, and Luke, before she could finish answering any of her questions, she had fallen asleep.

33

You're up early." Her mother glanced at the clock on the microwave as Sierra came into the kitchen the next morning, already showered and dressed for school. "I was going to let you sleep in a bit, on the theory that it wouldn't be the end of the world if you were late just once."

"Can you drive me to school early so that I can be there by seven?"

"Seven? Of course, but—" She broke off, her face registering recognition swiftly followed by distress. "Thursday. Choir. Oh, honey, I know how much you want to go with the rest of them on the trip, but I don't think Mr. Besser's going to budge. Mr. Lydgate can't fight him on this one. Unless your father . . . this DUI bombshell of his that he has ready to explode . . . But you know your father. He's going to do this thing *his* way, with *his* timing."

"That's not it." Sierra took a waffle from the box in

the freezer and put it in the toaster. "I know they're not going to let me go. I just want to be there at their last rehearsal. If Mr. Lydgate tells me I'm not allowed to be there, I'll go on to the suspension room."

"You're sure?"

Sierra nodded.

"Well, have some yogurt at least, along with the waffle. You can't go to school without some protein in your stomach."

As if Sierra needed protein so that her brain could process all that she was learning during eight periods of suspension.

But maybe protein would give her the strength and courage for what she was heading into school early to do.

The school choirs rehearsed in the auditorium, sharing the space throughout the day in alternating time slots with orchestra and band.

As Sierra walked down the dimly lit corridor from the front entrance to the auditorium—most of the lights hadn't been switched on yet—she could hear a couple of kids fooling around on the grand piano on the side of the stage, plunking out "Heart and Soul." Well, it was one step up from "Chopsticks."

Then she heard someone—a person who was obviously taking piano lessons—start to play a real piece of music. Sierra recognized it as the sonata of Mozart's that had the "Rondo alla Turca" in it. It had to be Celeste;

that was her piece for an upcoming Mostly Mozart kids' concert in February.

Waiting in the hall for a moment before going in, Sierra heard Celeste make a mistake and have to start the measure over again.

She was glad to hear her make it.

"Okay, singers, up on the risers," she heard Mr. Lydgate say with his usual heartiness, even at 7:00 a.m., when it was still dark outside, even on the day before a trip-of-a-lifetime that wasn't going to happen unless Mr. Besser budged. Or Colin budged. Or a miracle happened.

"I know the status of the trip is uncertain right now," Mr. Lydgate said, "but I still want you to give me everything you have this morning. We're going to belt our little hearts out. So let's get started, because Mr. Besser is planning to stop by to give us his send-off."

Someone said something that Sierra couldn't hear—probably Colin, with his soft voice.

"Well, I know Mr. Besser is hoping to be able to convince you to reconsider the boycott," Sierra heard Mr. Lydgate say. "Like me, he believes this is a fabulous opportunity for all of you to share what you've accomplished with music educators from all over the state. But I've said all I'm going to say on that subject. All right, let's warm up our voices."

Mr. Lydgate played the chords for the opening exercise.

"Mother made me munch my M&M's," seven voices warbled.

He struck the next-higher chord.

"Mother made me munch my M&M's."

If Sierra was going to do this thing, she had to do it now.

She came in quickly through the side door of the auditorium and slipped up onto the stage where the others were in formation on the risers, boy-girl-boy-girl. With seven instead of eight, one girl was missing on the end.

Still higher: "Mother made me munch my M&M's!"

Sierra slipped into her abandoned place on the end of the riser and joined the singing.

It took Mr. Lydgate a moment to notice she was there, though Celeste's gaze had fallen on her right away. Then his eyes lit up.

"Sierra! Welcome back!"

His face crinkled with relief, and he folded his arms across his chest in a gesture that clearly meant "Thank goodness."

Sierra realized that he must be thinking that she was back with Mr. Besser's permission, that Mr. Besser had lifted her suspension to save the choir trip.

"No," she said. "No—I'm not back. I wish I were, but I'm not."

He looked unbearably disappointed.

"Then, Sierra, I don't think . . . No. If you want to rehearse with us this one last time, I'm not going to be the one to tell you that you can't. That's Mr. Besser's job, not mine."

As if on cue, the door at the rear of the auditorium was flung open. Mr. Besser briskly strode up onto the stage.

He, too, didn't realize at once that Sierra was there, that eight students were arrayed on the risers instead of seven.

"Good morning, boys and girls!" Mr. Besser boomed, with his waggling eyebrows and wide, persuasive smile. "I don't want to interrupt your rehearsal. I want you to have time for this last important run-through of the program you're going to perform tomorrow as representatives of Longwood Middle School in Colorado Springs."

He was talking as if the boycott weren't happening, as if by his refusing to acknowledge it, it would cease to exist.

Then he, too, noticed Sierra.

She didn't give him a chance to rebuke her for being there. If she let him scold her, if she let him humiliate her in front of the rest of the choir, she wouldn't be able to do what she had come in early to do.

"Mr. Lydgate, Mr. Besser," Sierra said, coming down from the risers to face the choir as the two adult men were doing. "I know I'm not allowed to go on the trip. But there's something I want to say."

"Sierra," Mr. Besser said warily.

Sierra let her gaze fall on him coolly. The knowledge

of what had happened in his recent past, and of what was going to happen in his near future, gave her a power over him she hadn't had before. But she wasn't drawing on that power right now.

"I know some of you are upset about what has happened to me. You think it's unfair. Because it *is* unfair."

She didn't look at Mr. Besser to see if the muscles in his jaw were tightening, if his face was mottled with anger. Instead she made herself look at Colin, who was standing next to Celeste.

"I appreciate all you've tried to do for me. I mean, not for me, but to protest this unfairness."

She tried not to let sarcasm creep into her voice: *Believe me, I know you're not doing this for me.*

"But I want you to go on this trip. I want you to go. I love this choir. We've worked so hard this year, and the trip means so much to all of us—to me, too—and to Mr. Lydgate, who's been such a great teacher."

She hadn't meant to cry, but now she felt a wobble creeping into her voice.

"I just can't—I can't stand it—if—"

Mr. Lydgate laid a comforting hand on her shoulder.

"I just don't want anything else to be ruined," she finished in a whisper.

She couldn't let herself meet Colin's eyes, but she did let herself look at Celeste. Celeste was crying. Then Celeste stumbled down from the risers and hugged Sierra, hard. Sierra made herself accept Celeste's embrace.

Then the whole choir, including Colin, crowded around Sierra, hugging her.

Mr. Lydgate was wiping his eyes.

Only Mr. Besser stood apart from the group embrace. "Well!" he said, as they finally pulled apart.

For a fleeting moment, Sierra thought he might let her stay, let her go on the trip, that he might break his own inflexible rules just this once.

Then he said, "I guess Sierra and I should let you go on with your rehearsal."

But when the two of them reached the hall, and the auditorium door closed behind them, he turned to her and said, "Thank you."

Sierra was about to say, *I didn't do it for you, I did it for Mr. Lydgate, I did it for the choir,* but already, at 7:15 in the morning, she was too drained for any hostile confrontations with anyone. She wasn't like her father: hostile confrontations energized him and gave him strength.

But she also couldn't bring herself to say, *You're welcome,* or *That's okay.*

They walked in silence to the office. A couple of times Mr. Besser gave her a sidelong glance as if he was about to say something, but he didn't speak. What could he possibly say to her, given how wrongly he had acted, and how wrongly he was continuing to act?

When they reached the office, Sierra saw that Mrs. Saunders was seated at Ms. Lin's desk, and some new woman—with freckles and curly red hair like Anne of Green Gables—was seated at Mrs. Saunders's desk.

"This is Ms. Keith, who's temping for us this week," Mr. Besser said. "Ms. Keith, this is Sierra Shepard. She's one of our fine student leaders . . ."

Sierra watched him as he tried to figure out how to complete his habitual introduction. Would he show Ms. Keith the RULES RESPECT RESPONSIBIL-ITY RELIABILITY banner and compliment Sierra on her fine stitching?

Ms. Keith helped him out. "Hi, Sierra," she said. "I've read about your case in the paper. I'm sorry."

She said it without any apparent thought of whether it had been the wrong thing to say, of whether it might be taken as implying a criticism of her new boss, who was never to be criticized in any way.

Sierra smiled at Ms. Keith, relieved to see her break-ing the apparent rule: *Pretend you don't know what happened to Sierra Shepard; pretend you don't think it was unfair.*

"Thanks," Sierra said.

"Sierra," Mr. Besser said then, his voice as rich and smooth as if he had just drunk a long swig of cream straight out of the carton. "Would you step into my of-fice for a minute?"

Puzzled, Sierra followed him into the inner sanctum. She prayed as she sat down in the middle one of the three chairs facing his desk. *Dear God, please please please let*

Mr. Besser be about to give in. Maybe he hadn't wanted to announce his change of mind and change of heart in the choir room in front of everyone. Or maybe he had only come to his decision as they had walked back side by side: the principal who had hoped to save the choir trip, and the unselfish seventh grader who had actually saved it. Or maybe Ms. Keith's careless comment had made him finally see himself as others were seeing him.

She tried to keep the hope from shining out of her eyes in an eager, embarrassing way.

"Sierra," he said after a long moment of waiting, "you were the one who wrote that letter."

34

A voice came from inside Sierra, as if played by pushing a button on a CD player. "What letter?"

Waves of hot shame surged from her chest and her neck and washed across her burning face.

Was blushing like a lie detector test? Was blushing admissible as evidence in a court of law?

"Ms. Lin didn't write the letter, signed with her name, that appeared in yesterday's *Denver Post*. She claims she didn't write it, and I believe her. I have no reason to think that she hasn't been a wholehearted supporter of Longwood's zero-tolerance policies. And if she didn't write that letter, then there is someone else who did, and who sent it from her school e-mail account, on a morning that Ms. Lin was here alone because Mrs. Saunders had to be home on family business, during a time when her computer was left unattended."

Sierra said nothing.

"I called the *Denver Post* and spoke to their editorial page editor. They've printed a correction in today's paper, but of course the correction is buried away at the bottom of a page at the back of the paper, where ninety percent of the readers are likely to miss it."

The length of his speech had allowed Sierra to collect herself and try to get her face back under control.

She knew what her father, Gerald Edward Shepard, Esquire, would say: *Never admit anything.*

She didn't know what she, Sierra Grace Shepard, should say.

So she said nothing.

She forced herself to sit facing Mr. Besser and say nothing. She held his eyes—she wasn't the daughter of Gerald Edward Shepard, Esquire, for nothing—until he looked away, glancing down at his watch as if he had broken his gaze only because he was too busy to waste time in a staring contest with a seventh grader who was twenty-four hours away from expulsion.

"Okay, Sierra," he said. "Go on back. But if you decide there's anything you want to tell me, I'll be here in my office all morning."

Julio and Brad weren't there—their suspensions had finished yesterday—and at 8:30 Luke still wasn't there either. Sierra had brought a new book to read—a dystopian novel Lexi had recommended to her, as if her own life weren't dystopian enough. She didn't open it yet to start

190

reading. Her own thoughts bounced inside her head like kernels of popcorn in a popping machine.

What would Mr. Besser do next?

What *could* Mr. Besser do next?

Where was Luke?

Was Luke sick?

Or—this was the thought that made Sierra jump up from her lonely spot at the conference table and begin pacing. Had Mr. Besser summoned Luke into his office for a further round of accusations?

Would Luke tell?

When push came to shove—and hadn't push just come to shove?—would Luke testify against Sierra Shepturd? Would he derive his own satisfaction from bringing down the perfect girl who thought she was so superior to "kids like him"?

Sierra should have Googled "forgery" to find out what the penalties would be. It was the kind of question her father could have answered so easily—and the kind of question she could never ask him.

Footsteps down the hall.

Luke was there.

"Hey," Sierra said awkwardly. "I was getting worried. I thought that maybe . . . you were sick or something."

"Nope." Luke's eyes were bright, not with tears but with a wild excitement.

"Did—did Mr. Besser talk to you?"

"Yup."

The popcorn kernels exploding inside Sierra felt powerful enough to shatter their container and explode all over the suspension room floor.

Luke was apparently going to force her to ask the next question.

"And . . . ?"

Now his face turned back to its old sneering ugliness. "Don't worry. Little Miss Shep-turd is perfectly safe. She has nothing to worry about."

"Except for being expelled!"

"You won't be expelled," he said wearily. "Your father will save you, or the *Denver Post* will save you, or 9NEWS will save you. Someone will always come along to save you."

"But Mr. Besser—what did he say? What happened?"

"This time Luke Bishop saved you."

"So he asked—"

"He asked me if I wrote the letter to the *Denver Post.*"

"If *you* wrote it?"

"He said he asked you, and you hadn't confessed. He said that the four of us in the suspension room had the biggest motive and the best opportunity, and if it wasn't the good girl, then it was looking like it was one of the bad boys."

"He didn't really say that."

"Something pretty close to it."

"What did *you* say?"

"I said, yes, I did it. And I'm glad I did it. And I'd do it again."

35

L uke!"

His expression had changed from scornful anger to something that looked like hope. Hope that she'd look at him the way he had seen her look at Colin?

"Luke . . ."

Impulsively she hugged him, even though she didn't want to give him the wrong idea, the idea that she liked him, as in *liked* him liked him.

But as he hugged her back—he was taller than Colin and broader shouldered—as he stood, not hugging her anymore but just holding her, she worried that she might be giving him the *right* idea.

Then she pulled away.

"Did Mr. Besser believe you?"

"Oh, yeah. Or at least, he wanted to believe me."

"Did he say what he was going to do to you?"

"Guess who's going to have his own expulsion hearing?"

"You're going to be expelled?"

"This suspension I'm on now? It's my third this year. Fighting, fighting, swearing at a teacher. You can't have four suspensions in a year. That makes you a 'perennially disruptive student,' and they start expulsion proceedings."

Suddenly Sierra had a new suspicion.

"This suspension. Your third suspension. You did it on purpose. You wanted to be suspended."

To be with me.

"Maybe."

Luke grinned at her.

He had an incredibly appealing grin.

How could any girl at Longwood Middle School who'd seen that grin have a crush on Colin Beauvoir when she could have a crush on Luke Bishop instead?

"What else will happen to you? Like—"

She couldn't bring herself to say it: *criminal charges.*

"I'm supposed to apologize to Lintbag. That'll be fun, to have a chance to tell her some of what I think about her. I'll be sure to flash my Game Boy in her face when I do. But he didn't mention anything else. Expulsion is the main thing. Free at last, free at last, thank God almighty, I'm free at last."

"But—Luke."

"What?"

"I'm going to go tell him. The truth. I'm not going to let you get expelled for me."

"Why not? He already hates me. He doesn't hate you.

194

You're, like, his favorite student ever. I hate this school. The sooner I'm kicked out of here, the better. You don't hate it."

"Yes, I do. I hate it, too. I hate it more than you do!"

"You say you hate it now," Luke said. "But in a month, it'll be like none of this ever happened, and you'll be getting all A's again, and you'll be president of the school."

"There isn't a president of the school. There's a president of each class, but not of the school."

"See? You're the kind of person who knows that kind of thing. Okay, you'll be president of the Goody-Goody Brown-Nose Ass-Kissing Club."

Celeste could be president of that club. Sierra was through with that club forever.

"I'm not going to let you get expelled for me," she repeated.

"Look, I'm already going down."

"*I'm* already going down. *I'm* the one who's being expelled, not you. Just don't get suspended again, and you won't be expelled. And you could get A's if you wanted to."

"Maybe I don't want to."

She turned to leave.

"Sierra—don't."

She gave Luke another hug, and he hugged her back, tighter than he had before.

She headed down the hall to Mr. Besser's office, and to whatever would happen to her when she told him the truth.

36

He stepped out, hon," Ms. Keith said when Sierra's timid rap on the door of the inner sanctum produced no reply.

"But . . ."

Sierra had to talk to him this minute. If she hesitated even another thirty seconds, she might change her mind.

"Can I wait out here?" She pointed to the row of chairs beneath the appliquéd banner. "Instead of back there?"

Ms. Keith looked around, as if to solicit Mrs. Saunders's opinion on the question, but Mrs. Saunders was standing out in the front hall deep in conversation with a parent.

"Sure, hon," Ms. Keith said with a good-natured shrug. "I don't see why not."

Sierra sat down.

It was just over a week ago that she had been sitting

here in this very chair waiting to talk to Mr. Besser about the Zeroes Aren't Permitted program. Well, someone's life could certainly change forever in an instant.

"Do you know when he'll be back?" Sierra asked Ms. Keith.

"He didn't say. But I think he would have told us if he was going to be a while. Oh, here he is."

Mr. Besser strode into the office, grinning to himself, probably remembering some banter he had exchanged with a smart-mouthed eighth grader or a clever comment he had made to a teacher.

"Sierra would like to talk to you, if you have a couple of minutes," Ms. Keith told him.

His smile died away.

"All right, come on in, Sierra."

In the inner office, he sat down in his chair, and Sierra sat down in her chair.

"Luke didn't write that letter," Sierra said.

"I know," Mr. Besser said.

Silence for a moment.

"It was too well written," Mr. Besser said. "It wasn't written by somebody with Luke Bishop's grade in language arts."

Sierra couldn't bear to listen to Mr. Besser disparaging Luke in that way.

"Luke is smart! If he doesn't get good grades, it's because he doesn't want to!"

"I wouldn't call that a very smart choice, would you? But we're not here to discuss Luke Bishop; we're here to discuss you."

"It was just—Ms. Lin—she was so *mean* to me, and to Luke, to all of us. She took away his Game Boy, not just for one day, but for the whole rest of the *year*. And she treated me as if I had brought the knife to school on purpose, to *kill* someone, when I tried so hard to do the right thing and turn it in the second I found it. She made me feel like a criminal, and I'm not a criminal, I'm not. I've never done a criminal thing in my life!"

She broke off, remembering why she was sitting in Mr. Besser's office this very minute.

"Wouldn't you say," Mr. Besser asked, "that forgery is a crime?"

"Yes, I know it is, but it wasn't really forgery. It was just to get back at her because she had been so hateful and horrible."

"Sierra. The *Denver Post* published that letter. Over Ms. Lin's signature. As a member of the staff of this school. That letter is there in print for hundreds of thousands of people to read as a representation—a misrepresentation—of the views of a member of our Longwood Middle School community."

Sierra had been prepared to be contrite, to say over and over again how sorry she was, but talk of "our Longwood Middle School community" made her suddenly think of the Beautiful Mountain community. They knew what it meant to be a community. In a real community you didn't destroy a member of the community just to uphold a policy that never should have been established in the first place.

For a few moments Sierra sat silent. Then she managed to say, "Now that you know that Ms. Lin didn't write the letter, is she going to get her job back?"

"I didn't fire Ms. Lin. She quit. And after you explain to her what happened—and you *are* going to explain to her what happened—she certainly has the right to decide if she wants to retract her resignation. But I don't think she will. She is very upset."

Not just about my letter. She's upset that you lost your cool and yelled at her about it in that horrible demeaning way.

"I'm sorry," Sierra said.

And now she truly was sorry.

I never meant for any of this to happen!

She waited for a minute to see what Mr. Besser would say next.

He gazed out the window. Sierra's gaze followed his. It was starting to snow again, the first few thick flakes floating lazily through the air like tufts of down from a torn pillow.

Maybe he would never say anything, and she would never say anything, and they would sit in his office for the rest of the morning wordlessly watching the snow falling onto the winter-brown grass.

Luke would wonder what had happened to her, Luke who was willing to be expelled for her sake.

Sierra spoke first, losing the silence contest just as she had won the staring contest an hour ago.

"So what happens now?" she asked. She tried to make it sound as if she were asking out of mere curiosity, as if she were asking how much accumulation was expected from the morning's snowfall.

"I don't know," Mr. Besser said.

The answer surprised her.

"What do *you* think should happen?" he asked.

The question surprised her even more. It had been a long time since anybody at Longwood Middle School seemed to care about what she thought her fate should be.

"I should apologize to Ms. Lin," Sierra said slowly.

Mr. Besser nodded.

Sierra couldn't tell if he was nodding in agreement or just nodding to show that he was listening.

Sierra continued. "And the *Denver Post* already knows, and they've printed the correction, even if not that many people will read it."

Please don't make me tell the Denver Post! She couldn't bear to have her crime be the lead story on the nightly news.

"And for punishment." Sierra still couldn't read Mr. Besser's impassive face. "Well, if I'm already getting expelled for something I didn't do, or didn't mean to do, then maybe that punishment can be for this, too."

That was all she had to say.

Mr. Besser's phone rang. He picked it up. "Put whoever it is on hold," he said into the receiver.

He looked back at Sierra.

"Why did Luke Bishop say he wrote the letter if he didn't?"

The way he asked the question made Sierra know—or at least think that she knew—that Mr. Besser wasn't going to call the police and have her taken away in handcuffs.

"I think he likes me," Sierra said.

Mr. Besser gave Sierra a real smile this time.

"Yes, I'd say he does. All right, Sierra, go on back."

Apparently their conversation was over, and he had accepted her suggestions for how to proceed.

"What about Ms. Lin? Should I call her? I don't have her phone number."

"Mrs. Saunders can give it to you."

He picked up the phone, where the red hold button was still blinking.

"And, Sierra, you know I'm letting you off easy on this one because I do regret, truly regret, everything that has happened."

"I know," Sierra said.

But as she left his office, she wanted to ask him, *Do you, really? Do you? Because if you did, you could still stop the hearing tomorrow. You could. You could.*

37

Luke was standing by the suspension room door waiting for her. He didn't hug her this time, but when they sat down at the conference table side by side, he reached over and took her hand.

"What are they going to do to you?" he asked.

"It's going to be okay. Because of everything else that's happened. Because I'm already being expelled anyway."

"So they're not doing *anything*?"

Was Luke annoyed at this latest evidence of yet more unfair favoring of Little Miss Shep-turd?

"I have to apologize to Ms. Lin."

"So are you just supposed to call her, or what?" Luke asked.

"He didn't say. I think you're supposed to apologize to someone in person. You know, like when you send a thank-you note, it's supposed to be handwritten, not typed on the computer."

Luke stared at her.

"Don't you ever write thank-you notes?" she asked.

"Thank-you notes for what?" was all he said.

"Well, anyway, I guess I'll call her and explain that there's something I want to tell her in person, and I'll see if she's willing to meet with me."

"Can I come, too?" Luke asked.

"What do *you* have to apologize to her for?"

"Well, I was there when you did it. Besides, I just want to see what she says."

"I don't think apologies are a spectator event, where people come and watch," Sierra told him.

But now that Luke had offered to come, all Sierra could think about was how much less scary the whole thing would be if he was there. Unless he laughed during it. Or otherwise wrecked it.

But he wouldn't.

Would he?

Mrs. Saunders gave Sierra Ms. Lin's phone number without asking why she wanted it. Maybe she already knew.

"Do you know where she lives?" Sierra asked.

Was she going to have to ask her mother to drive her there?

"Just over in the apartments at Fourth and Aspen. It's walking distance. She walked to school most days."

Back in the suspension room, Sierra took out the cell phone that she was forbidden to use during school hours.

Having survived the conference with Mr. Besser gave her new confidence as she dialed Ms. Lin's number. Or maybe she was just getting used to living in an alternate reality, doing things that in her previous life she could never have even imagined.

"Hello?" Ms. Lin said. On the phone she sounded as prissy and officious as she had at her desk at Longwood Middle School.

"Ms. Lin? It's Sierra Shepard."

A long pause on Ms. Lin's end.

"There's something I need to talk to you about."

Another long pause.

"It's about something I did. And, if it's okay, I'd like to talk to you in person. Like today? After school?"

Another pause. The whole conversation was turning out to be: Sierra speak, silence from Ms. Lin, Sierra speak, silence from Ms. Lin.

"I could come over to your house. I mean, your apartment. Or meet you somewhere. Like in a coffee shop? The one by—"

"You can come to my apartment," Ms. Lin said. "After school is fine."

Before Sierra could ask for the apartment number, or if she could bring Luke Bishop with her, Ms. Lin had hung up.

"So?" Luke asked her. "What did she say?"

"We're going after school. Today."

Sierra got the apartment number from Mrs. Saunders—
182—and permission to call her mother to say that she
wouldn't need a ride home today. She could walk home
after the apology. It was a long walk—perhaps two
miles—but doable, especially as it had stopped snowing by lunch, with only one or two inches total of new
snow. On the phone, she had told her mother she couldn't
talk longer right now, but she knew she'd end up telling
her everything sooner or later; she almost always did.

There were no reporters waiting outside school today.
Good.

Sierra had wondered if Luke would hold her hand as
they began walking toward the Oak Grove Apartments,
the way Colin had held Celeste's hand yesterday.

He didn't.

Sierra felt ashamed at her relief, at her realization that
she would have felt embarrassed if Luke had held her
hand in public, where anybody could see. She wasn't ready
for other people to know that she liked, of all people,
Luke Bishop.

And then Sierra did yet another thing that she would
never have imagined herself doing.

Casually, as if she hadn't given the matter any thought
at all, she reached over and caught Luke's hand in hers.
His face lit up with surprised pleasure as his gloved hand
closed around her mittened one.

Apartment 182 was a ground-level unit, with a door open-ing onto the snowy courtyard in the rear of the complex, facing the mountains.

Still holding Luke's hand, Sierra rang the doorbell with a mittened finger of her free hand. Maybe the sight of two seventh graders holding hands would make Ms. Lin even madder. But there was no way that Sierra was going to let go of Luke's hand now.

The door opened.

"Sierra, Luke," Ms. Lin said, "come on in."

"Should we take off our shoes?" Sierra asked. "They're snowy."

"Yes, please do."

Sierra let go of Luke's hand as she removed her shoes and hung her coat on the coat stand. But she took it again as they sat down together on the floral-patterned couch facing a matching floral armchair.

The first surprise of the visit was that Ms. Lin was wearing jeans and a sweatshirt that had a picture of a zebra and the word KENYA printed beneath it. In the office Ms. Lin had worn only pantsuits that looked as if they had come from a Proper Secretary catalog.

The second surprise was that the only word to de-scribe Ms. Lin's apartment was "cozy." A gas fire burned in the fireplace. A teddy bear—a teddy bear!—sat in a small rocker beside it. On the wall hung a yellow-and-blue quilt that looked homemade. And the view of the mountains from the large picture window was breath-taking.

"Have you been to Kenya?" Sierra asked once Ms. Lin had seated herself in the armchair, not that they were paying a social visit. But she did want to know.

"Three times."

"Wow," Sierra said.

Ms. Lin didn't volunteer any details about her trips. She also hadn't offered them any tea or set out a plate of cookies.

"I'm here to apologize for something," Sierra said.

"I thought as much."

"I'm the one who wrote that letter to the *Post*."

"And I helped," Luke added.

"No, *I* did it."

She knew she wasn't supposed to provide the explanation she had offered Mr. Besser: *But I just did it because you were so mean and hateful, such a horrible petty tyrant.*

"And I shouldn't have done it. I'm sorry. I really am. So that's what I came to say. That I'm sorry."

"How were you able to get into my e-mail account?" Ms. Lin sounded more puzzled than angry.

"It was the day Mrs. Saunders wasn't there. Because of her son's wisdom teeth. And you had gone to the bathroom or something. And you had taken Luke's Game Boy. And we wanted to get it back, so we went over to your desk. And you had your computer on, opened to your e-mail."

Sierra kept on babbling since she didn't know what else to do.

"So you didn't have to quit. And I know Mr. Besser would give you your job back. I know he would."

"What makes you think I want my job back? Do you know what I said to myself as I walked out of there for the last time? Free at last, free at last, thank God almighty, I'm free at last."

That she said exactly the same words Luke had said when he was contemplating his own expulsion made Luke laugh out loud.

"You think that's funny, don't you," Ms. Lin said. She still didn't sound angry. "Well, let me tell you, I'm glad to get your apology, but after today I'd prefer never to see another middle school student again as long as I live. Or another middle school principal."

Ms. Lin didn't look at Sierra and Luke as she spoke.

"I've spent eighteen years in a job I hated," she went on, "and yesterday I took some of my ample savings—I call it my blood money—and I bought myself a ticket for a monthlong vacation trip to Nairobi."

"Nairobi?" Sierra asked.

"The capital of Kenya. I guess Mr. Besser's astonishing educational initiatives haven't reached as far as teaching world geography. I'm leaving in two weeks."

"I hope you have a good time," Sierra said.

"Oh, I will. Believe me, I will."

"I guess we should go now."

"I guess you should."

Sierra and Luke stood up.

"Your apartment is pretty," Sierra said.

"Thank you," Ms. Lin said. "Now go, both of you. Just go."

Sierra and Luke put on their coats and their shoes and left.

38

Luke offered to walk home with Sierra.

"But you live in the opposite direction," she protested.

"So?"

"Oh, Luke," she said. "Right now I need to be by myself for a little while to sort things out, okay?"

And he didn't get huffy or touchy. He just said, "Sure, I'm cool with that," and gave her another hug.

Sierra started her long, cold walk. She knew that all she would have to do was call her mother on her cell phone and her mother would be there in five minutes, but she needed some time to think.

The hearing was tomorrow morning at ten.

Tomorrow her father was going to squish Mr. Besser like a bug, and Sierra was going to find out if the superintendent of schools was going to expel her or let her stay at Longwood Middle School.

So one way or another, this had been her last day ever

of suspension. By Monday she'd be either reinstated or expelled. And she had spent her last day in suspension falling in love with Luke Bishop!

If she was expelled, she'd be starting either at Beautiful Mountain or at some other, more "academic" school chosen by her father. He hadn't mentioned anything about what school he'd like her to attend once she was expelled from the public school district. Apparently he was so confident he'd prevail at the hearing that it wasn't worth his time to consider any alternatives. Probably, if he had to, he'd pick Braxton Country Day School, the fancy private school north of town. Sierra would never fit in with the snobby rich kids there.

But even if she was reinstated at Longwood Middle School, it would never be the same. She'd never again be Sierra Shepard, fine student leader. She'd be Sierra Shepard, who was almost expelled for bringing a knife to school. Sierra Shepard, who didn't get to go on the big choir trip. Sierra Shepard, who had already missed a week of work in every class and would never be able to catch up. Sierra Shepard, who hung around with Luke Bishop.

Sierra's fate would be decided tomorrow morning.

Though her fate had really been decided the minute she opened her lunch bag at school on Wednesday, January 23. No, even before: when she had picked up the lunch bag that morning. And Mr. Besser: his fate had been decided when he had told that other principal that zero tolerance meant *zero* tolerance, with no exceptions ever. No, earlier, when he had drunk too much and gotten behind the wheel of a car on the evening of November 29. Ms. Lin's fate had been decided when she stepped away from her desk on Monday, January 28, to go to the bathroom.

And Sierra's parents: their fate had been decided when her father had laughed during her mother's play. If that hadn't happened, they wouldn't have gotten married, and Sierra wouldn't have been born, and she wouldn't be twelve years old right now and ready to find out whether or not she was going to be expelled from Longwood Middle School.

Tomorrow at ten.

39

At eight-thirty the next morning Sierra awoke to find her bedroom filled with the dazzling brightness of sun after snow.

Still not fully awake, she checked her phone: five texts. She had turned it off the previous evening, unable to face any messages from anybody.

Celeste: *Good luck today. I wish you were going with us.*

Colin: *I hope you win. You deserve to.*

Lexi: *Em told me about C and C. Are you okay?*

Em: *OMG, was that you walking with Luke B? Call me!*

Luke: *Suspension sucks without u. Miss u bad.*

Sierra wasn't going to text anybody back. But then she did text Luke: *miss u 2.*

In the kitchen, her father was seated at the breakfast table, handsome in his gray attorney suit, reading *The New York Times.* He looked up from the paper to give her a confident smile.

"In less than two hours, all this will be behind you, sweetheart."

Then he seemed actually to see her, still in her pajamas. "You're not dressed yet. Wear something preppy. The school uniform look. Do you have a plaid skirt? White blouse? Dark blazer?"

Her mother was wearing a dress—less long and flowy and Beautiful Mountain–ish than most of her other clothes. Maybe Sierra's father had coached her, too, on what to wear to a daughter's expulsion hearing.

"Breakfast first," her mother said. "Eggs today, I think. How about a small omelet with spinach and cheese?"

"I'm not really—"

"Yes, you are," her mother said. "You need to eat."

Apparently it wasn't a good idea to go to an expulsion hearing on an empty stomach.

"Where is the hearing?" Sierra asked.

"At the Board of Education complex," her father replied. "That big new bunch of buildings they built after the last bond issue. Over on Twenty-ninth Street and Pine."

"Who else will be there? Besides us, and Mr. Besser, and the superintendent?"

"Probably the attorney for the school district, because this has become such a high-profile case." A flicker of pleasure passed over his face: he knew who was responsible for its having become "such a high-profile case."

"And the press, of course. It's a public hearing, thanks to the 'open air' provisions of the board charter."

He wasn't exactly rubbing his hands together in smug anticipation of the media's likely reaction to his brilliantly timed little bombshell, but he might as well have been. Instead he straightened his already straight tie and ran his hand through his neatly trimmed gray hair as if readying himself for military inspection.

Sierra's mother set the omelet and toast in front of her, as well as a small glass of orange juice. Sierra took a sip of the juice. She didn't think she could handle something eggy and cheesy and spinachy right now.

When she was little, she used to have to leave the family room during any movie that had scary music in it. Even if it was a kids' movie with a guaranteed happy ending, she couldn't stand the suspenseful parts that happened on the way to the happy ending; she had to skip over all those tense, awful, nail-biting, knuckle-whitening bits. She'd hide out in the hall until it was safe to return and watch the closing scene of the faithful dog reunited with his little boy master.

"You haven't even touched your breakfast," her mother scolded.

Sierra took one nibble from one half of her piece of toast.

"Take just three bites of the omelet. Two bites."

Sierra took one bite and tried not to gag on it, washing it down quickly with another swig of the orange juice, which tasted suddenly bitter, so acidic that she could feel it burning a hole in the lining of her stomach as scary music pounded inside her head, music for the scary movie of her own scary life.

At the Board of Education building, her father led the way down the hall to the small auditorium where board meetings—and high-profile expulsion hearings—were held, without needing to consult any building floor plan or ask anyone for directions. He carried a slim, expensive leather briefcase. Sierra knew at least one thing that was in that briefcase: police reports concerning Thomas Alford Besser forwarded from the State of Massachusetts.

Sierra and her mother walked hand in hand.

Sierra was wearing the same red plaid skirt she had worn on the day it all happened, together with a navy-blue blazer she had found at the back of her closet. Her father had been right that it made the perfect costume for acting the part of Unjustly Accused Honor Student.

Yesterday afternoon, as soon as she got home, Sierra had told her mother about her visit to Ms. Lin.

She hadn't told her father.

Her mother hadn't said, *Oh, Sierra, how could you?* or *Sierra, I'm disappointed in you,* or *Sierra, I hope you learned your lesson.* She had just hugged her and made her hot tea so that Sierra could warm her frozen hands on the steaming mug and hold it against her chapped cheeks.

At the back of the auditorium stood three television cameramen with all their equipment. Sierra recognized the three reporters who had interviewed her over the past week.

"Good luck, Sierra!" the blond reporter called over to her as Sierra walked through the door with her parents.

Sierra gave a small, cautious wave in return.

Mr. Besser was already there, talking to two other men: the lawyer for the school district and the superintendent of schools?

She tugged at her blouse to make sure it was tucked into the waistband of her skirt. She smoothed her hair, held back from her face with a white headband that matched her blouse.

Should she smile or look serious? Serious was probably best. She didn't want the superintendent of schools to glare at her and ask, *And what are you smiling at, young lady?*

That was the kind of thing Ms. Lin would have said.

Sierra sat between her parents in the front row on the right side of the little aisle leading from the front to the back of the room. Mr. Besser and the shorter, stouter man sat on the other side; the shorter, stouter man must be the school district lawyer. The thin man, Abe Lincoln–gaunt, sat down at the small table on the raised podium in the front of the room, so he had to be the superintendent, Mr. Van Ek.

"I suppose we might as well begin," Mr. Van Ek said.

Sierra's mother's hand tightened around hers.

Mr. Van Ek made some opening remarks about due process of law, too boring for Sierra to listen to, even though they probably were extremely significant for her fate. She could feel her father's focused attention on every word.

"Tom?" Mr. Van Ek said then.

Mr. Besser stood up and approached the table.

For the first time Sierra noticed that Mr. Besser and her father were both wearing almost identical dark gray suits and white shirts. The only difference was that her father wore a regular long tie, while Mr. Besser wore his trademark bow tie.

Mr. Besser began by saying things Sierra had heard before, oh, so many times before. How important the new zero-tolerance policy had been to Longwood Middle School. How every student who enrolled in the school knew exactly what the policy said. Every single student and every single parent had signed a statement consenting to the policy.

"Here's the form signed by Sierra Shepard and by her parents, Gerald and Angie Shepard."

So the school had actually kept those dumb forms everybody had to fill out and sign at the beginning of the school year.

"Do I believe that Sierra deliberately brought that knife to school? No. But does the presence of that knife in her possession on school grounds constitute a violation under our zero-tolerance policy? Yes. Is this an offense that calls for mandatory expulsion? It is. Do I deeply regret the necessity for this final step in this unfortunate case? Yes, I do."

Sierra could feel her father's whole body growing tense; she could feel him drawing himself upright, leaning forward with squared shoulders, clenched jaw.

She wanted to excuse herself, say she needed to go to the bathroom, flee to the hall.

But now Mr. Besser was speaking directly, not to Mr. Van Ek, but to her.

"Sierra."

She looked at him.

"Sierra," he said again. "What you did."

Blood pounded in Sierra's temples: Was he going to betray her publicly for her forgery, tell three television reporters what she had done to Ms. Lin?

"Yesterday. About the choir trip."

Sierra took a ragged, gasping breath.

She realized that she hadn't told her parents, not even her mother, about the speech she had made to save the Octave's trip. It seemed to have happened many years ago.

Mr. Besser gave Sierra a shaky smile, matching the unexpected tenderness in his tone, as if his voice might start to wobble the way hers did sometimes.

"Right now," Mr. Besser told Mr. Van Ek, "our a cappella choir, the Octave, is on its way to perform at the Colorado Music Educators convention, an enormous honor for our school. This is a trip that was on the verge of being canceled because of a student protest on behalf of Sierra, a trip that would not be taking place right now if Sierra hadn't come in yesterday morning to encourage—to implore—the rest of the choir to go without her. I haven't known many students who could be so selfless, who make rules, respect, responsibility, and reliability their own personal concern. Sierra, I thank you."

Sierra's father had apparently had all he could stand.

"I presume," he said, rising to his feet to interrupt Mr. Besser, "that the point of this hearing isn't to commend this fine student leader but to expel her. Do I have that correct?"

"Yes, but I also want to take this opportunity to thank Sierra publicly for what she did for this school, for all she has done for this school, now that she has to be leaving us."

Sierra saw that her father had already taken his sheaf of papers from his briefcase.

"So you are going to continue to make the case for expelling this fine student leader, who has done so much for this school in so many ways, despite one tiny, innocent mistake that she sought to correct immediately upon its discovery."

He spoke as if he needed to be completely certain on this one crucial point before he said what he was about to say next.

Mr. Besser nodded. "Regretfully, I am. In the circumstances, I have no choice."

"Well, then." Sierra's father remained unsmiling, but she knew that within his heart was wild, fierce exultation. The moment he had been waiting for had arrived at last, the moment for squishing Mr. Besser like a contemptible, hypocritical, soon-to-be-obliterated insect.

"It just so happens that I have some information to share with our esteemed superintendent of schools, and with our vigilant ladies and gentlemen of the press, information that I consider to be somewhat, shall we say, relevant to this case, or at least might be perceived to be relevant by those with a highly attuned sense of irony."

Sierra forced herself to look at Mr. Besser. His ruddy face was several shades paler than it had been five minutes ago, and the kindly, regretful smile he had been beaming toward Sierra remained frozen in place, like the smile one might see on a corpse.

Not that Sierra had ever seen a corpse, or ever wanted to see one.

But it felt as if she were looking at one right now.

40

Daddy."

She was next to him, tugging at his arm.

"Daddy. I'm—I don't feel well. I think I'm going to be sick."

Mr. Van Ek was on his feet. Sierra could tell from his quick motions that he didn't like it if people threw up in his special room for expelling students.

"Take her outside for a few minutes," he instructed Sierra's father.

Sierra's mother had jumped up, too. "Here, lean on me," her mother said. "Let's get you out in the hall, or to the ladies' room. I knew you needed to eat a proper breakfast."

Outside the door of the hearing room, Sierra dropped down onto a bench.

"Put your head between your legs if you're feeling dizzy or light-headed. Or do you need to throw up? We passed the ladies' room on the way in, it's not far from here."

"I'm okay," Sierra said as her mother, sitting beside her, smoothed her hair. "I just felt—I can't—"

Her father, still standing, looked mildly annoyed.

"Talk about bad timing," he grumbled. "Now he knows what's coming. Did you see his face? Now we've lost the element of surprise. Not that he can figure out how to save himself during a five-minute recess. Because there isn't any way that he can save himself. Okay, sweetie, are you ready to go back in? Angie, see if you can get her a paper cup of water, or a Coke from the vending machine."

"I'm not going back in," Sierra said.

"But, honey," her mother said, keeping her encircling arm around Sierra's shoulders. "I think you have to. It's your hearing, our hearing. We all need to be there."

"That's not what I meant. It's Mr. Besser. Telling what he did. Telling everyone. It's too—awful."

"Oh, give me a break," her father said. "What he's doing to you—that's not awful? Being a pompous hypocrite is one thing. Being a pompous hypocrite who is destroying a little girl's life is another thing. I'm the father of that little girl, and I'm not going to allow him to do it unpunished."

"Daddy."

He was looking at his watch. Maybe he was wondering

how long it was going to take to destroy Mr. Besser, given this unfortunate interruption, and if he was going to have to call his secretary to reschedule his late-morning appointments. Sierra waited until he looked back at her to continue.

"Daddy, I'm not a little girl."

Not anymore.

"And my life's not being destroyed."

She had never felt as fully alive as she did right now.

"Expelling someone for an innocent mistake?" her father said.

"He knows it's wrong," Sierra said. "He just can't back down. Because he got locked in—"

"And needs to save face," her father finished the sentence for her. "But he's going to find out that, guess what, it didn't work, and he's never going to be able to show his sorry face in this school district again. And that's going to be the best thing that has happened to this school district in a long, long time."

"I don't want you to do it," Sierra said.

"I'm your father, and I have to do what I think is right."

Was it right to destroy someone's career because he was a pompous hypocrite? Because he was a pompous hypocrite who had driven a car while under the influence of alcohol and might have killed someone?

Why did it matter so much, being right?

"Daddy, if you tell them about Mr. Besser, I'm going

to transfer to Beautiful Mountain, whether I get expelled or not. If you try to make me stay at Longwood or go to Braxton, I'll fail every class on purpose."

Her father looked as stunned as if Cornflake had quadrupled in size and pounced on the neighbor's pit bull.

"And who, may I ask, is going to pay your tuition at Beautiful Mountain?"

He had better not add that her mother couldn't afford to pay it from her income as an unpublished playwright.

"You are," Sierra told him.

He glanced over at his wife, his eyes steely with anger. "Angie, this is your doing."

Her mother's eyes were steely, too. "Having a strong-willed, assertive, feisty daughter is *my* doing?"

"This Beautiful Mountain crapola is your doing."

The attorney for the school district poked his head out into the hall.

"Is she feeling better now?" he asked Sierra's father.

"I'm feeling fine now, thank you," Sierra said.

"Then the superintendent would like you to come back in so that we can finish this up."

Sierra led the way back into the hearing room. She didn't look to see if her father was following her, or to monitor what expression he had on his face.

In the end, her father would do whatever he chose to do.

"Mr. Shepard, you were about to present some new information for my consideration," the superintendent said once Sierra and her mother were seated again. Her father remained standing in front of the table.

"I have here in my briefcase," her father said, "some highly relevant news reports."

Sierra stared down at her lap.

"News reports about how other school districts across the country with strict and absolute zero-tolerance policies have handled similar cases."

She let out her breath.

"In Tennessee: exception made for a student who had a toy gun in a Civil War diorama. In Minnesota: exception made for a student who brought in a razor blade to cut out paper snowflakes for a collage project in art class. In Oregon: exception made for a student who had her mother's prescription medication in the wrong lunch bag by mistake."

He paused for effect.

"In the wrong lunch bag by mistake," he repeated. "I have seven more cases I could present, instances in which sanity and common sense prevailed over bureaucratic rigidity and foolish face-saving by school officials."

Here her father did look directly at Mr. Besser with a barely restrained smirk.

"If you'd like, I can continue sharing them with you."

"That won't be necessary," Mr. Van Ek said. "Thank you for your very helpful research, Mr. Shepard.

Mr. Besser, do you have anything that you would like to add before I make my ruling in this case?"

Mr. Besser didn't look at Sierra's father; he looked directly at Sierra, a long inscrutable gaze, and then rose to face Mr. Van Ek.

"I believed, and continue to believe, that I had no option under my school's stated policies—policies, I repeat, that were consented to in writing by every student and every parent at this school—no option but to enforce those policies conscientiously to the letter of the law. If 'zero tolerance' means anything, it has to mean precisely that, however lax other school districts may have been in their interpretation: zero tolerance. *Zero* tolerance."

Maybe now Sierra's father would wave that other news report in Mr. Besser's plump, bland, self-satisfied face.

"But," Mr. Besser said, "I can understand and appreciate the grounds for ruling otherwise in this particular case, especially given the outstanding contributions of this particular student. So I will respect your ruling, Mr. Van Ek, whatever it might be."

Mr. Van Ek nodded judiciously.

"Thank you, Mr. Besser. While my office has the right to review the arguments put forward here for seven days before handing down a ruling, I don't see any benefit in prolonging the resolution of this unfortunate case."

Sierra willed her heart to keep on beating. Was there hope for her after all?

"I believe that the new zero-tolerance policies put in place under Tom Besser's leadership of Longwood Middle School have been significantly responsible for making this school one of the highest-performing middle schools in the state of Colorado."

Mr. Van Ek didn't look toward Sierra and her parents as he spoke in defense of all that Mr. Besser had done.

So next Monday Sierra would be starting at Braxton Country Day School, if her father could expedite the admission and registration process in her case. Which she had no doubt he could do. She didn't know if she could make good on her threat to force him to let her attend Beautiful Mountain.

"But I also believe," Mr. Van Ek said, "that we should follow the precedents presented to us by Mr. Shepard from our peer districts and permit some very few exceptions. Indeed, Mr. Besser, I would urge you to craft a more carefully worded policy that makes clear that zero tolerance will not apply to accidental violations when the student takes immediate steps to notify school officials of the mistake, as Sierra Shepard did in this case."

He paused.

"Sierra can stay at Longwood Middle School. She should receive no academic penalties for the time she has already been absent from class, and she should be given every opportunity to make up the work she was forced to miss so that she can continue in her record of outstanding academic achievement."

It was over.

Her mother, who had been gripping Sierra's hand throughout Mr. Van Ek's speech, swept her into a hug.

Her father was grinning. He had, after all, won, and winning was what he loved more than anything else in the world.

No, not more than he loved Sierra. For her, he had given up the exquisite pleasure of squishing Mr. Besser like a bug. Her mother was right. Love was still the chink in her father's armor.

She watched her father shake Mr. Van Ek's hand and then offer his hand to Mr. Besser as well. Winners could afford to be generous. He even gave Mr. Besser a playful slap on the shoulder, as if in promise that he held no hard feelings toward the man he had been about to ruin.

Then Mr. Besser came over to Sierra and her mother.

"I'm glad that you'll be back," he said warmly. "I couldn't be more pleased with the superintendent's decision."

Did Mr. Besser know that she had saved him?

But if she had saved him, he had also saved her.

"Sierra!" The blond reporter from 9NEWS was calling over to her.

"Go to your adoring fans," Mr. Besser told her, gesturing toward the cameras at the rear of the room. Then he leaned over and whispered in her ear, "Speaking of adoring fans, you can do better than Luke Bishop, you know."

Sierra didn't reply. She was going to text Luke as soon as she was in the car—Luke and Em and Lexi, and maybe even Celeste and Colin, too. And then she was going to go home and cuddle Cornflake and print out her Mayan culture report and spend a few hours just lying on top of the quilt on her bed, staring up at the canopy over her head. She couldn't face returning to school until Monday.

"Oh, and Sierra," Mr. Besser called after her as she was heading over to the waiting reporters. "If you can get a ride from one of your parents to the Springs, I believe you can get there in time to take part in the choir concert. They're taking the stage this afternoon at four."

"I can drive her," Sierra's mother said. Sierra gave her mother a grateful hug.

She thought of the banner hanging in the front office with its appliquéd inscription.

RULES
RESPECT
RESPONSIBILITY
RELIABILITY

Now she could add REGRET.

And RETHINKING A WHOLE BUNCH OF THINGS.

And most of all RELIEF.

For the first time, she was glad that the *R* in RELIA-
BILITY was a little bit crooked.

Everything in her life was a little bit more crooked
than it used to be.

And right now, as far as Sierra was concerned, that
was completely and totally and wonderfully okay.

Go Fish!

SQUARE FISH

ZERO TOLERANCE
by Claudia Mills

Discussion Questions

1. In the novel's opening scene, Sierra is waiting in the school office to speak to the principal about her idea to implement the ZAP (Zeroes Aren't Permitted) program at her middle school. Sierra is mildly annoyed by the crooked "R" in the word "Reliability" on the banner promoting the school's creed: RULES, RESPECT, RESPONSIBILITY, RELIABILITY. How does this initial scene in the story define Sierra's character for the reader?

2. Sierra's personality is further defined by the list of goals she makes for the semester. Sierra appears to be a perfectionist, but her goals also hint at some of her social concerns. How does her goal "don't let people push you around" foreshadow how she chooses to behave as the story progresses?

3. Sierra makes a pivotal decision in the cafeteria when she discovers that she has mistakenly taken her mother's lunch bag to school instead of her own. If you were faced with the same situation, how would you respond to it?

4. The principal, Mr. Besser, is also placed in a challenging situation when he finds Sierra in his office after the lunchtime discovery. How do you think the presence of a visiting principal affects how Mr. Besser deals with Sierra's infraction?

5. Sierra's view of her crush, Colin, as well as her close circle of friends shifts during the course of her battle with the school. Colin in particular changes from soulful poet to champion and ultimately to boyfriend of someone else. How does the reaction of Colin and Sierra's friends in Leadership Club and choir shape Sierra's trouble with the school administration?

6. The zero-tolerance policy at the middle school clearly outlines the consequences for students who break the rules—mandatory expulsion. Sierra is dismayed and her parents are enraged at the thought of Sierra having to leave Longwood Middle School for an alternative school. What was your emotional reaction as you read the section of the story describing the initial meeting between Mr. Besser and Sierra's family?

7. Sierra is placed in in-school suspension until her expulsion hearing. The detention room is populated with troublemakers. Sierra is reminded that her mother always said that everything happens for a reason. "Maybe the reason Sierra had gotten a completely unfair in-school suspension was so she could learn that bad kids weren't as bad as she had thought they were, that they were actually pretty nice." What lessons about people and the nature of fairness does Sierra learn in the detention room?

8. Sierra's father is a lawyer and decides that media attention will help Sierra's case with the school. How does the media's coverage of Sierra's plight help and hinder her battle with her school's zero-tolerance policy?

9. At the beginning of the novel, Sierra is a studious, rule-abiding leader in her middle school. Sierra shows a darker side of her character when she uses Ms. Lin's email to send a letter to the editor of the newspaper. In contrast, Luke breaks from his troubled behavior to support Sierra. Both Sierra and Luke are multidimensional characters with the ability to be both tough and soft, rebellious and obedient. How do multifaceted characters add to a story with a black-and-white theme of zero tolerance?

10. Sierra mulls over the concept of fate towards the end of the story. Was she fated to bring the wrong lunch bag to school that dreadful day? Was Mr. Besser's fate sealed when he shared the zero-tolerance policy with the visiting principal the day of Sierra's infraction? Was Ms. Lin's fate decided the day she stepped away from her desk long enough for Sierra to use her email? Was Sierra's dad fated to laugh at her mom's play in a case of mistaken enjoyment of her mom's writing? Does the concept of fate take away from the characters' responsibilities for their actions in the story?

11. As Sierra's expulsion hearing is resolved, she feels that "everything in her life [is] a little bit more crooked than it used to be." Why is the idea of imperfection and subjectivity so powerful to Sierra after all she goes through in the story?

Common Core State Standards addressed by the discussion questions and activities in this guide include:
CCSS.ELA-Literacy.RL.6.1, 6.2, 6.3, 6.5, 7.2, 7.3, 8.2, 8.3
For more information about the Common Core, visit www.core standards.org.

The discussion questions and following activities in this guide were created by Leigh Courtney, Ph.D. She teaches in the Global Education Program at a public elementary school in San Diego, California. She holds both masters' and doctoral degrees in education, with an emphasis on curriculum and instruction.

ACTIVITIES

🍎 Search for examples of people in the news who have "done the right thing." Share these current events with your friends or classmates and discuss any celebrations or controversies surrounding the do-gooders' actions.

🍎 Think about the need for some sort of rules to govern behavior and ensure student safety in school. List the pros and cons of a zero-tolerance policy at school.

🍎 Examine your list of pros and cons for a zero-tolerance policy at school. Decide which side you can best support in an argument. Use the list to help build a persuasive essay either supporting the implementation of a zero-tolerance policy or contradicting the need for such a policy in a school setting.

🍎 Imagine how the incident of Sierra bringing a knife to school and the subsequent controversy appeared through the eyes of the principal, Mr. Besser. Write a journal entry from the point of view of the principal. Do you think he was conflicted about his administrative responsibilities? Was he disappointed in Sierra? Did he feel anger towards the legal actions Sierra's father set in motion?

🍎 Examine the cover of the novel. How does this illustration encapsulate the events of the story? Create your own cover illustration. Display your class's book covers on a bulletin board in the classroom or in the school library.

🍎 Complete a T-chart comparing Sierra's interests and attitudes before the incident of bringing a knife to school and her interests and attitudes after she felt the sting of her school's zero-tolerance policy.

🍎 Illustrate what you consider to be the most important scene in the story. Share your illustration and reasoning for the scene's importance in the novel with a partner or the class at large.

GOFISH

CLAUDIA MILLS

Larry Harwood

What did you want to be when you grew up?
I always wanted to be a writer. The only other thing I even considered being was president of the United States. In third grade, I made a hundred-dollar bet with Jimmy Burnett that I would be president someday, but now I'm starting to think maybe Jimmy Burnett is going to win that bet.

When did you realize you wanted to be a writer?
When I was six and my sister was five, my mother gave each of us one of those marble composition notebooks. She told me that my notebook was supposed to be my poetry book, and she told my sister that her notebook was supposed to be her journal. So I started writing poetry, and my sister started keeping a journal, and we both found out that we loved doing it.

What's your most embarrassing childhood memory?

Oh, there are so many! One day in third grade, I decided to run away from school, and I made a very public announcement to that effect. But when I got to the edge of the playground, I realized I had no place to go, so I had to come slinking back again. That memory still makes me cringe.

What's your favorite childhood memory?

We vacationed every summer at a little lake in New Hampshire, and I remember sitting out on the lake in a rowboat, writing poems and drawing pictures and making up stories about imaginary princesses with my sister. Those were very happy days.

As a young person, who did you look up to most?

I mostly looked up to characters in books who were braver and stronger than I was, like Sara Crewe in *A Little Princess,* who loses her beloved father and has to live in poverty in Miss Minchin's cold, miserable garret, but never stops acting like the princess that she feels she is in inside. I also looked up to Anne of Green Gables for her spunk in breaking that slate over Gilbert Blythe's head.

What was your favorite thing about school?

It's sort of weird and nerdy to say this, but I loved almost everything about school, and during summer vacations, I'd even cross off the days until school started again. Best of all, I loved any writing assignments and being in plays. In fifth grade, I played the role of stuck-up cousin Annabelle in our classroom play of *Caddie Woodlawn*, and that was wonderful.

What was your least favorite thing about school?
Definitely PE! I was always terrible at PE. I just couldn't do any of the sports, and one time the fourth-grade teacher made the whole class stop and look over at how terribly I was doing this one exercise. I still hate her for that.

What were your hobbies as a kid? What are your hobbies now?
Well, writing, definitely, and reading and taking long walks. Hey, those are my same hobbies now. The only new hobby I've added is obsessively checking e-mail.

What was your first job, and what was your "worst" job?
My first job was working in the junior clothes department at Sears. Back then, three girls worked in one department: one to work the cash register, one to oversee the dressing room, and one to tidy up the clothes racks. I loved tidying up the clothes racks, buttoning up the dresses that needed buttoning. I loved buttoning one dress so much that I bought it, and then found that once I had it at home I had no desire to button it at all anymore. My worst job was being a waitress. I would have done all right if I could have handled just one table at a time, from drinks to salad to main course and

then dessert, but my brain could not handle juggling all those different tables at once.

How did you celebrate publishing your first book?
I don't remember celebrating it. Now that I look back, I wish I had. It's a very special moment.

Where do you write your books?
I write all my books in longhand, lying on the couch, using the same clipboard-without-a-clip that I've had for thirty years, always using a white narrow-ruled pad with no margins, and always using a Pilot Razor Point fine-tipped black marker pen.

What sparked your imagination for *Zero Tolerance*?
A number of years ago, I read a news story in the local paper about a private school in a nearby town where a ten-year-old honor student was expelled for bringing a knife to school by mistake in her mother's lunch. The story stayed with me, even though I didn't follow the media coverage to find out what actually ended up happening to the student in question and whether the principal's judgment was reversed. I couldn't stop thinking about how someone's world would be turned upside down by being treated so harshly for an innocent error so promptly corrected. What would this do to this kid's understanding of herself and her world?

Have you ever been in a situation like Sierra?
I have not. But I've spent much of my life trying very hard to be a "good girl" who was liked by teachers and principals. I remember once being sent out into the hall for talking, when the actual culprit was someone else, and how terrible—terrifying, even—it felt to be accused and punished with no ability to defend myself.

Was zero tolerance a difficult subject to write about?
In my other life, I've spent twenty years as a professor of philosophy at the University of Colorado, teaching and writing about all different kinds of issues in ethics. So this kind of ethically rich topic has a natural appeal for me.

Do you think the situation would have been handled differently if Sierra had been in high school?
I don't know. What I do think, and this is a difficult thing to have to say, is that it might have been handled differently—and worse—if Sierra hadn't been a member of a privileged socio-economic group. She has a powerful attorney father to defend her. What if she had been a kid whose parents had fewer resources? Or who was already judged as lesser, more likely to be involved with weapons, because of her race or ethnicity?

What do you hope readers will take from this book?
While I do think zero-tolerance policies in general are a bad idea, that's not the main thing I hope readers will

take away from reading *Zero Tolerance*. It's that people—including *us* —are more complicated than they—and *we* —might seem at first sight. Even basically good people can do some harmful and destructive things. We don't fully know who we are and what we are capable of until circumstances test us. And what we find out then might not be what we wanted to know. But sometimes we end up stronger and better because of it.

Of the books you've written, which is your favorite?
I don't have a favorite. My books feel like my children; each one has such a huge piece of my heart in it. So I wouldn't want to hurt their feelings by loving one of them more than its brothers and sisters.

What challenges do you face in the writing process, and how do you overcome them?
By far the biggest challenge is learning how to accept, and even to welcome, criticism. I hate criticism and always want everybody to love my books from the very first draft. But the only way to grow as a writer, and to produce the best possible book, is to listen to what critical readers tell you, and then rewrite, rewrite, rewrite.

Which of your characters is most like you?
Each one is like me in some way, or maybe I become more like that character as I write about him or her. I think overall the two who are most like me are Dinah in the Dinah books and Lizzie in *Lizzie at Last*. Lizzie is so much

like me that I even dedicated the book to myself: "For the girl I used to be."

What makes you laugh out loud?
I always laugh out loud if somebody is trying to do something in an oh-so-serious way and then something goes hideously and publicly awry. That kind of thing makes me howl.

What do you do on a rainy day?
Write and read, of course!

What's your idea of fun?
Writing and reading!

What's your favorite song?
Gosh, I have so many. I guess I'll go with "Here Comes the Sun" by The Beatles.

Who is your favorite fictional character?
Betsy Ray in the Betsy-Tacy books by Maud Hart Lovelace

What was your favorite book when you were a kid? Do you have a favorite book now?
It was and still is *Betsy and Tacy Go Downtown* by Maud Hart Lovelace, which I consider to be the finest novel in the English language.

What's your favorite TV show or movie?
I don't watch much TV. My favorite movie, in recent years, is *Julie & Julia*; I loved watching both women develop as writers.

If you were stranded on a desert island, who would you want for company?
I'd be happy with pretty much anybody. In elementary school, the teachers would keep moving my desk so I'd stop talking to the person next to me, but then they found out that I would be happy talking to anyone.

If you could travel anywhere in the world, where would you go and what would you do?
I'd like to live in Paris, in a garret, and write, and be very poor, and make money by selling flowers on the street corner.

If you could travel in time, where would you go and what would you do?
I'd go back to Amherst, Massachusetts, in the 1850s, and walk by Emily Dickinson's house, and see if she would lower a little basket out the window to me with a fresh-baked muffin and a freshly written poem in it.

What's the best advice you have ever received about writing?
Brenda Ueland says, in *If You Want to Write*, that writing is supposed to be fun, and that if we allow ourselves to let it be fun, stories and poems will just keep pouring out of us. I think she's right.

**Do you ever get writer's block? What do you do
to get back on track?**
I don't, really. My secret is to write for a short, fixed time—
usually an hour—every single day. That way I never get
burned out from writing, and I never get far enough away
from my story that I lose my momentum.

**What do you want readers to remember about your
books?**
I always try to have my main character learn a small but
important truth about how to make his or her life better.
I know when I think back to favorite books I read a long
time ago, it tends to be some little, trivial-but-fun detail
that sticks in my head.

What would you do if you ever stopped writing?
Oh, I hope I never do! But I do love reading almost as
much, so I guess I'd just read, read, read. Or teach
writing, which I do already and love doing.

What do you like best about yourself?
I am very good at being cheerful. I have all kinds of
strategies and techniques and lists and mantras that I use
to cheer myself up when I have hard things to deal with in
my life. I think I have a gift for making myself reasonably
happy.

**Do you have any strange or funny habits? Did
you when you were a kid?**
I chew my pen or pencil as I write—I always have. Once,

a few years ago, I chewed my pen so hard while I was writing that I broke my tooth and had to spend five hundred dollars at the dentist to get it fixed.

What do you consider to be your greatest accomplishment?

I'm proud that I've written over forty books while always working full-time at another demanding profession (being a university professor of philosophy).

What do you wish you could do better?

I wish I could cook. The meals at my house are horrible. I pretty much live on English muffins with butter and orange marmalade.

What would your readers be most surprised to learn about you?

My favorite food is candy, particularly seasonal candy: candy corn at Halloween, those little Conversation Hearts for Valentine's Day, Cadbury Creme Eggs at Easter.

APPLE NACHOS

By Alethea Allarey of the Read Now Sleep Later blog
readnowsleeplater.com
Inspired by the book *Zero Tolerance* by Claudia Mills

When Sierra gets in trouble for breaking her school's zero-tolerance policy against weapons, her mom keeps trying to keep her spirits up. She's affectionate and loving, but most noticeably (as most good moms do) she keeps feeding Sierra comfort foods. As the book goes on and Sierra becomes more and more disgusted by her own actions, she develops aversions to particular foods. I can't say I blame her! If only she hadn't brought that knife to school by accident . . .

Below, I've included some ideas for apple nachos. If you're a kid, have an adult help you with the chopping and heating parts. You can vary the amounts as you wish, but for a lot of the toppings, just a tablespoon of each will do. Recipes for the sauces follow. And please, remember to leave the knife at home!

Enjoy!

Credit: Alethea first found the basic recipe on Allyson Kramer's blog.

APPLE NACHOS

Ingredients:
An apple, any variety
A lemon
Assorted toppings

Equipment:
A knife
A cutting board
A mixing bowl
A serving plate
(or a container with an air-tight lid if you're taking it to school)

Makes 1-2 servings

1. Wash and dry an apple. You can peel the skin off if you want to, but I like to keep it on unless it's a variety that has a bitter or waxy skin.

2. With an adult's help, chop the apple into quarters. Carefully cut out the core with the stem and seeds, then slice each quarter into thinner slices. These are your "chips."

3. Cut the lemon in half and squeeze the juice into a bowl.

4. Toss the apple chips in the lemon juice and let them soak for a minute. This will stop them from turning brown right away. Drain and pat the apple chips dry with a paper towel.

5. Arrange the slices on a plate and add your choice of toppings. You can drizzle the sauces on or put them on the side for dipping.

6. Eat it right away, or take it to school with you.

Suggested Toppings:

The Sweet Sierra *(the sweet and sour variation)*
Dulce de leche or caramel sauce + raisins + mini chocolate chips + shredded coconut

The Media Circus *(the nutty variation)*
Peanut butter sauce + raisins + chopped pecans + banana slices

The Principal Besser *(the school lunch variation)*
Nacho cheese (yes, apples taste great with cheese!) + diced tomatoes, olives, and jalapeños (optional)

The Gerald Edward Shepard, Esquire *(the fine dining variation)*
Extra-virgin olive oil + balsamic glaze or vinegar + pine nuts + crushed, dried basil or oregano + Parmesan cheese (You can toss a little crushed garlic in there if you're really feeling brave)

The Cornflake *(the French toast variation)*

Maple syrup + crumbled, shredded wheat or other cereal + cinnamon sugar

The Angie Shepard *(the tough cookie variation)*

Cookie butter sauce + slivered almonds + dried cranberries

The Comfort of Friends *(the hot chocolate variation)*

Chocolate syrup + mini marshmallows + whipped cream*

You're going to want to eat this right away, unless you have access to a refrigerator at school. You can also toast this combo after adding marshmallows, but before adding the chocolate syrup and whipped cream!

Sauces:

Caramel sauce (based on Ree Drummond's ingredients)

2 Tbsp brown sugar
1 Tbsp half and half, heavy whipping cream, or milk
$1/2$ Tbsp butter
Tiny pinch of salt
A few drops of vanilla extract

In a small saucepan over low heat, stir together all the ingredients except the vanilla. When the sauce has melted and blended together (about 1 minute), stir in the vanilla. Turn off the heat and keep stirring all the while to help it cool down. When it is no longer very hot, pour over apple nachos.

Peanut butter sauce

2 Tbsp peanut butter, smooth or crunchy
1 Tbsp half and half, heavy whipping cream, or milk
1 Tbsp white or brown sugar
Tiny pinch of salt
1 tsp maple syrup or light corn syrup

In a small saucepan over medium heat, stir together all the ingredients until well blended. Turn off the heat and keep stirring all the while to help it cool down. When it is no longer very hot, pour over apple nachos.

Cookie butter sauce

2 Tbsp cookie butter, regular or crunchy
1 Tbsp half and half, heavy whipping cream, or milk
1 Tbsp white or brown sugar

Tiny pinch of salt in a small saucepan over medium heat, stir together all the ingredients until well blended. Turn off the heat and keep stirring all the while to help it cool down. When it is no longer very hot, pour over apple nachos.

Tips:

- Try using a Granny Smith apple for the Sweet Sierra variation since it's a little tart—it balances out all the sweet stuff and represents Sierra's character changes throughout the book. Gala apples or any kind you have available can be used for all the rest.

- Mallow Bits were used for the hot chocolate variation, but use regular mini marshmallows if you're going to toast it.

- You can serve this for a big crowd—place toppings in serving bowls with spoons or ladles, and let everyone make up their own combination!